QUANTUM ENTANGLEMENTS

QUANTUM ENTANGLEMENTS

NOAH SERIES

JORDYN KROSS

Scarlet Parlor Press, LLC

Find all of Jordyn's books:

Melting Hearts Series

Prequel Novella - Jack's Frost

(free for newsletter subscribers)

Book 1 - Winter's List

Book 2 - Xmas Angel

Book 3 - Shattered Ice

Dirty Daisy Mystery Series

Book 1 - Dirty Daisy

Book 2 - Hell Hath No Furry

Uhraervi Brothers

Open Enrollment

Hung with Care

Pole Position

Nonfiction

Demystifying the Beats

Published by Scarlet Parlor Press, LLC

Library of Congress Control Number: 2023915869

ISBN: 978-1-959691-01-3 (ebook) | 978-1-959691-04-4 (paperback)

Editor: Jenny Rardon

Cover: Brandi Doane McCann

Dedicated to my grandfather, Dr. Kaiser Kunz, professor of physics, particularly quantum mechanics.

CHAPTER 1

2123 AD
Spaceport, New Mexico, USA

All hands, mandatory meeting.

Something was wrong. Leandra Richards wiped her perspiring palms on her black slacks as her trainer's words beat a warning in her gut. On stage, five of the Nostradamus Outerspace Advancement of Humanity—NOAH—project coordinators conferred with whispered intensity. Nothing could be more important than continuing the training for their upcoming mission and the physical demands of life in space. The other scientists, including the women from her training team, filed into the auditorium. From the way they chatted with each other and relaxed into the navy-blue padded seating, they were clueless. Didn't they understand the significance of an urgent, unscheduled meeting?

None of them came to sit with Leandra, but they'd only been together for a matter of weeks. Her focus was on learning everything for the mission, where it should be. Everything that could save her life once she was hurtling through space in an unknown galaxy. Besides, making friends wasn't her best skill. She could worry about making friends after the teams were assigned in a few months. If there still was a mission.

The head of the mission went to the microphone. "I'm sure you're wondering why we've called you all here." She paused, allowing the chatter to go silent. "There's been...a change." The other leaders didn't react at all. Their blank faces ratcheted up Leandra's internal warning bells from chiming to clanging. "We've organized the final teams. The launches are scheduled to begin in the morning."

What?

No.

Her breath froze in her lungs as her heart raced.

The chatter of her fellow trainees started up again in hushed staccato tones.

Of all the possible reasons for the unscheduled meeting, premature launching hadn't even been on her list.

Leaving so early was impossible. Leandra had volunteered for NOAH because it was a research mission. A vision for the future should Earth be unable to recover from the "good intentions" of long-dead experts. Research implied no modifications to the plan. No surprises. No emergencies.

She still had months of critical life-saving training before she would be prepared to leave the planet and everything she'd ever known. Her instructor had promised her more time to practice donning her survival suit. Leandra shot her shaking hand into the air.

"Yes, Dr. Richards?" The fatigue in the woman's voice was noticeable, but she wasn't the one getting on a rocket. Leandra was.

"Based on the fact that we were already following a severely compressed training course, there is no possible way we can be prepared to launch tomorrow." Leandra clasped her hand, raising her chin. They couldn't. Astronauts trained for years, and Leandra and the others had months, except they didn't. Everyone in the room must've been questioning the deviation from their plan, even if she was the only one brave enough to voice it.

The former astronaut who ran mission safety stepped up beside the director. "You've received the critical information and physical training for the mission. The remaining weeks would have been drills primarily and almost no new information provided."

"Almost?" Leandra blurted out. Almost wasn't *none*.

"Each team has been assigned a fully trained captain—an experienced astronaut with years of training. They will answer questions and provide guidance regarding the space travel aspects of your mission. You will continue to train aboard the ships."

Leandra couldn't be expected to go into space for the rest of her life—to preserve the human genome and terraform new planets—with incomplete training. She shifted in her chair, gripping the arms. Besides, an expert was only helpful if you asked the correct questions. "Why is the launch being moved up?"

The director leaned into the microphone. "Overnight, Yellowstone had a significant uplift on the south rim of the caldera. If it erupts, the event will devastate..." She dropped her eyes and swallowed. "It will have devastating effects here at the Spaceport and..."

And all over the planet.

Leandra's chest tightened. Earth had been destabilizing in multiple ways for quite some time, something the people in the room knew more about than your average Joe, but the cataclysmic event wasn't supposed to be in her lifetime. "What about—"

The director spoke over Leandra's question. "I'm afraid any other questions must be submitted by email. We have a tight launch schedule and need to assemble the final teams."

Email. Right. As if the answer would matter when she was being shot into space strapped to a giant firework.

Names were called. First the married couples, nine of them. Then individual names. All seemingly in the target reproductive age range. They were balancing the teams' genders and scientific specialties from what Leandra could tell. Did the directors falsely believe that the couples would reproduce in space? Was it possible? Or even a good idea?

Having a family was a dream she'd abandoned long ago, no matter how much the decision still stung. As the ecosystem continued to deteriorate, even her proven genetic engineering and fertility protocols had diminishing efficacy. Perhaps that's why they were sending couples instead of just frozen sperm. That and their need to fill specific scientific roles likely required recruiting at least some men.

The unknowns of gestation in space and the general decrease in human fertility meant the odds of any of the teams naturally carrying a baby fully to term were nearly zero. That's why so many other scientific specialties were involved in the project. In addition to trying to terraform multiple planets, the human genome would be spliced into other species, or other species would be spliced into human DNA. New life forms—ones designed for the environments they encountered—could be established. At least, that's what she'd been told.

Not for the first time, she wondered why she'd agreed to participate. The change in the launch schedule only added to her doubts that she could do anything but fail on this mission.

But she had to go because what if she was the key to figuring out how to make this preposterous plan work?

CHAPTER 2

"Dr. Leandra Richards." The director focused her gaze on Leandra as if reading the doubts that clouded her mind. Leandra made her way to the stairs of the stage, glancing toward the exit a few meters away. With a deep breath, she placed her foot on the first riser and went to join the team leader, his wife, and two others who had already been assigned to her group.

The single man held out his hand. "Officer Iver Garnier. Welcome to the Japheth team. I'll be your captain."

His smile should have put him in films. Leandra tipped her head so that her dark hair hid most of the scar that circled her cheek, hooking the edge of her mouth. She shook his hand. "Captain?"

"Space Force. Six years." He was thick with muscles, cocky with attitude, and darkly handsome with jet-black hair, brown eyes, and a slightly shadowed jaw. "I also have an electrical engineering degree from Georgia Tech."

Leandra was saved from trying to generate the correct response by a slender woman with creamy skin and amber eyes, her dark hair cut in a pixie style. She was the embodiment of the chicness Leandra had always envied.

"I'm Mahi Tengan. I'm the medical doctor for this group."

Leandra clasped her petite but strong hand. "Leandra."

Meeting the strangers she would spend the rest of her life with was odd.

Leandra realized she had missed the announcement when a man with curly blond hair bounded toward them. He slapped palms with Iver. "Hey, mate. Charles Carson, marine biologist."

Not quite as useful as a doctor or pilot, but okay. And what was an Australian doing on the American teams? Australia had its own ships ready to deploy.

Charles introduced himself to the team lead next—all the men, of course.

"Barret Myers," the lead responded and indicated his wife. "Rabiah Nabarro, plant geneticist."

"And he's my bug guy." Rabiah smiled. "Can't have one without the other."

Rabiah was surprisingly appealing with her short stature, wiry ash hair, and dark eyes. Her skin was pale for someone with the tight musculature of a gardener. And she looked at her mousy husband—too tall, thin, with thick glasses and watery blue eyes—with such adoration, as if the sexy Australian wasn't appealing at all. Leandra instantly liked her.

"Shea Davidson," the director called.

A fairly tall, pear-shaped woman with thick sandy hair and wireframe glasses approached their group. Her wide mouth hinted at a smile. Instead of her name, she announced, "Computer engineer. I'll be running the modeling and simulation for the terraforming projects. Have they said anything about the equipment we'll have on board? I requested some serious qubits to get the data we need."

A computer engineer familiar with quantum computing made more sense than a marine biologist. And Leandra appreciated her work ethic. She wouldn't mind spending time with Shea and learning more about the models she used to generate her data.

Before Leandra could introduce herself, another name was called—one that sent her heart racing and made her gut clench.

Harlan Johnson.

It couldn't be.

He was disgraced in the scientific world, deservedly so.

Maybe... She scanned the auditorium. There. Standing in the back was the only man who ever broke her heart and the very last person she'd recruit for a project of this importance. He still looked like a god, with his tall, athletic body, tightly clipped afro, and piercing brown eyes. Eyes that locked on her as he smirked and waggled his fingers before sauntering down the stairs to the stage. Fingers that had once been inside her. Heat crept up her cheeks. Her pussy clenched with an unwanted reminder of how nice his cock was, too.

As he came closer, she glanced around for an escape, but her gaze was drawn back to him. He winked, sending a violent electric surge through her limbs. The nerve of him to act like everything was a joke. She had to get away from him, transfer teams. She craned her neck as the last names were being called to see if any team was short a person.

No. Everyone was grouped up, smiling and making introductions. She spotted other genetic engineers—all men. She couldn't trade with them, or the teams would be unbalanced. But if she didn't transfer, she'd be trapped for the rest of her life, trying to save humanity with a man who hated her—with good reason—a man she would never trust.

"This is a terrible idea." The words washed out of her on a breath.

Shea leaned in close. "All the best ones are."

Leandra swallowed hard. Harlan neared the stage. No time

to run. After all, the mission was bigger than Leandra's issues with a past lover. She squared her shoulders. They'd both have to act like grown-ups. Be professional. Scientists with a greater purpose. It would work out.

Barret greeted Harlan. "Gang's all here now. Next step, getting in the tin can and going where no one has gone before to save the empire or something like that." He chuckled at his hodge-podge of historical space references. "Only reason I'm going is to keep the wife company. When you find a woman who can put up with your affinity for cockroaches, you follow her anywhere. Guess they thought hanging on to her showed enough good judgment that I would make a decent team lead."

Unlikely. Leandra was far more qualified, having been CEO of her business for several years. But no one asked her.

Rabiah smiled indulgently at her husband. "My plants can't survive without your insects. Both will be crucial to our terraforming mission. No point trying to save humanity without plants *and* bugs."

As a couple, they were adorkable. A pang of wistfulness, of what could have been, shot through Leandra. She shook it off. Nostalgia and what-ifs had no place in this mission.

The teams began filing out of the auditorium, following the director. When Leandra got to the unmoving Harlan, he leaned down and whispered, "Were the media interviews really necessary? My co-author duped me, but I wasn't the asshole."

Before she could pick her jaw up and respond, he turned his back to her, striding away on long legs. She sure wasn't the asshole for doing the right thing. *As if.* It's not like she owed him some personal phone call. He'd certainly avoided calling her when he should have. How typical that he would drop a bomb like that and walk away before giving her a chance to respond.

His hair might be shorter, his voice deeper, and his body

may have shifted from boy to man, but he hadn't changed a bit since college. Still completely focused on himself to the exclusion of all others. She'd do well to keep that in the forefront of her mind because it was her brain that was in charge, not her body demanding more of his sexy voice, more of his touch, and more of his cock deep inside her.

Nope. Not going to happen. She'd fallen for his brand of sexy before. A failed experiment, and she was too wise to repeat that mistake.

CHAPTER 3

Harlan leaned against the back wall of the drab common room for their floor in the dormitory. Members of the team relaxed on the L-shaped couch and in club chairs. Team Japheth wasn't scheduled to leave for a few more days. The first two shuttles had gone up without a hitch. One team was already on their way to the wormhole...or ERQ bridge. Same thing—a volatile hole punched through space, dependent on quantum entanglement to hold it open, one that could collapse at any moment. It would be a hell of a ride—if they made it.

Barret walked in and beelined over. "I wish we could just go already. These daily workouts are killing me."

Harlan made an appropriate noise of agreement. He enjoyed the workouts, but the entomologist was obviously not big on physical activity.

"You don't seem excited to go either." Barret pushed his glasses up his nose.

"Either?"

"Kind of a losing proposition. If we fail, the human race is gone. If we succeed, how many more planets will we destroy?"

Well, wasn't their team lead just a ray of fucking sunshine. "Fair point. But I'm up to seeing what we can do. Maybe if we're able to hybridize successfully, humans won't be such assholes."

"Unlikely. On both hybridizing and not being assholes."

Barret's wife waved him over. "We're just about to start a movie. Sit by me."

Barret grinned and sauntered to her, as if the man had any game. But he had a wife, which was infinitely better than game, especially when they were heading into the unknown. It would be a lot easier to face knowing there was someone on board who cared if you lived or died.

Leandra stood with the remote control aimed at the wall-mounted television, adjusting the video display colors and brightness. She still had a phenomenal physique. Only a few inches shorter than his six feet, her long brown hair cascaded like a river down to the middle of her back. Her breasts, the perfect handful, were still high and tight. His palms itched at the memory of holding her naked golden flesh. She had a body built for marathon running and marathon sex.

Harlan shifted as the replay of their time in college teased his cock.

"Everyone ready?" She faced the group, catching Harlan's eye. Her gaze narrowed and frosted over.

Harlan smirked. She couldn't let anyone else control anything, not even a simple movie night.

She spun and sat between Iver and Charles, pulling her hair forward to hide the scar she was so self-conscious about. A scar that was barely noticeable unless she was smiling or laughing. And in Harlan's admittedly limited time with her, he'd only seen her laugh once.

The movie opened. It was an old one, a sequel to some action adventure in space. How appropriate for a team about to give up their lives, risk everything, and eventually die in the cold void with strangers. Except Leandra couldn't be counted as a stranger—not after he'd been inside her. Can't hate someone you don't know. If he'd kept his dick in his pants all those years ago, he probably wouldn't be on this team or part of this project. He'd still have his career. She'd gone out of her way to sabotage him because they'd fucked.

Never again.

He scanned the team members once more. Dr. Tengan—Mahi—was cute in a fairy kind of way, with her pale skin, slight build, and short hair that framed her face. And there was Shea Davidson, the computer geek. She wasn't pretty in the traditional sense, with her thick hair cut in a bob, a nose slightly too large for her face, and a farm-girl physique. But she had a wide smile that met her sparkling blue eyes, and Harlan had nothing against a woman with an ample backside. Not that he had to start a relationship with anyone. Theoretically, they should connect with the other ships in about three years, docking them together to form a space station. It wouldn't be the first time he'd gone that long without a partner. And no partner was better than the wrong one, especially when there would be no running away if the romantic connection fizzled.

Harlan slipped away for some air. They'd be locked inside for the foreseeable future all too soon. The sun dipped in the desert sky. Streaks of brilliant orange dashed across the fading blue. He left the sidewalks and crunched his way across the decomposed granite sands, away from the lights of the building. A chill raced through him as he gazed at the distant mountains shrouded in dark-purple shadows. Earth was beautiful. There would never be another planet as graceful, tender, and fierce as her. He bent and scooped up a handful of the still-warm crushed rock, letting it sift through his fingers. No matter what they did, they were out of time. A miracle couldn't save the planet, and there was only a slim possibility they might save the human race.

The first stars peeked out of the darkening horizon, familiar in their obscurity. Soon he'd be traveling beyond the stars and planets he'd gazed upon so often. Slapping his hands together to brush the dust away, he wandered back to the building toward his room.

The mission was his final opportunity to recreate his discredited research and prove that, even though lies had compromised his data, his theory was sound. Although no one else would ever learn of his success, Leandra would know. She'd be unable to deny that his method of mapping first, editing the genomes, and then fertilizing would produce more viable embryos than the increasingly lackluster, dated methods she refused to deviate from.

Despite the fact he'd be forced to spend his life with the woman he dreamed of far too often and for far too long—a woman who'd pursued him in school, a woman who'd hated him ever since—going was the right thing to do. He'd always done what he thought was right, even if it hurt people in the short run, even if they didn't understand. Leandra wouldn't be the scientist she'd become if he hadn't cut her loose after their one epic night of perfect connection.

Passion like theirs could make people do stupid things and give up their dreams. In his experience, that only led to resentment. Yeah, best to keep his cock tucked away or in his own hand as a last resort. He was plenty familiar with that solution. In fact, a little solo action might be the perfect way to release the tension while he waited to find out when they'd launch. And so what if he pictured Leandra—she'd never know.

CHAPTER 4

LEANDRA PAUSED the movie when the NOAH director came into the community room.

"Team Japheth has been cleared to launch in the morning. Get your rest, folks. Tomorrow, you have the chance to become superheroes." She turned and left.

A stunned silence hung over the room. Suddenly, it was all too real. Barret and Rabiah, the first to recover, said goodnight and left.

Leandra glanced between Iver and Charles. "Do you want to—" She held up the remote.

They shook their heads.

Dr. Tengan stood. "See you bright and early."

Leandra clicked off the video.

Iver stood, all smiles. "All right, you guys. Get some shut-eye for the big day. This is what we trained for. Time to make the magic happen."

"You got it, mate." Charles slapped hands with Iver, and they walked off toward their rooms, making testosterone-fueled statements to each other as they faded away.

Leandra stared at the tiny buttons on the remote control. She could press pause on her own life like she had for the movie. No one could make her get on the ship. The crossroads loomed before her. What had once been theory transformed with a few words into stark reality. On the one hand, if she didn't go, she'd be trapped on a dying planet with no way of contributing anything meaningful. On the other, she had an indeterminate lifespan in a metal tube with six other strangers and a man she still lusted after, despite how much he hated her.

"It's a bit startling."

Leandra snapped her gaze up.

Shea stood near the window with the curtain drawn back. The overhead light made it impossible to see through the glass.

"I don't think I've ever been so uncertain about my future," Leandra confessed.

"Yeah, it's all fun and games until the scenario becomes reality." Shea dropped the curtain. "I have to say I prefer modeling and simulations to real life as a general practice."

"I didn't think I did. I even read nonfiction because novels are so much supposition and coincidence." Leandra placed the remote on the faux-wood table perfectly aligned with the edge. "I've spent my entire career making sure real human babies get born." Even if they weren't hers. "Part of me feels like I'm giving up if I leave. That none of what I did to this point had any purpose."

"It's a funny thing. You're hired by the exact organizations that made the shitty decisions that led to disaster to prove what everyone already knows is wrong. There weren't enough ways to manipulate the models to excuse the bad mandates they made to *save* the planet." Shea crossed the floor toward the exit. "And now, I'm leaving the planet to run more impossible scenarios about the minimum characteristics for an unknown, unoccupied planet to be a potential for terraforming."

"Sounds like a lose-lose choice."

Shea shrugged. "The impossible scenarios have much more

potential than the actual reality here. And besides, I'll be my own boss. See you in the morning."

Leandra stared at the empty doorway. Shea was right. They had the choice of certain failure or nearly impossible success. Certain failure came with a lot of comfort—her home, videos, wine, maybe even a man. Well, that last one wasn't likely, but there was a chance. Leandra didn't see herself getting attached to the cocky space pilot or the Aussie water boy, but there would be others once the ships met up in a galaxy far, far from home. Anybody but Harlan.

Harlan.

If she didn't get on the ship, humanity would be left in his hands. He'd already proven incompetent at managing a team and unable to discern faulty data. Could she really abandon the fate of humanity to him?

She swallowed and stood. Time to get some sleep for the big day tomorrow because she was getting on the damn rocket. And she and Harlan would just have to pull up their grown-up pants and forget the past and their—okay, *her*—lingering attraction for the rest of her life. She had an impossible job to do, and no one was more qualified or capable of seeing it through. If there was even the slightest possibility of this Hail Mary attempt working, she had to try.

CHAPTER 5

Leandra finished locking away her newly fertilized cell cultures in the small incubator. After months on the spaceship, she was fully adapted to the lower gravity that the ship's quantum created. It beat the hell out of the zero gravity they'd had on the station orbiting Earth as they transferred to their long-haul ship designed to connect to the other ships like children's building blocks. The sooner she could create a sufficient number of blastocysts, the better. They had to start incubating the fetuses that would be trained as the next generation of scientists to continue the NOAH work.

There were only two artificial gestation devices on board and an infinite number of causes for failure to overcome. Artificial gestation was something Leandra had avoided in her own practice, preferring natural gestation. But with only four women on board and none of them looking to be low-gravitation guinea pigs, mechanical devices would be the only possible method.

But a new challenge would soon be upon them, and she dreaded it. Crossing the Einstein-Rosen-Quantum bridge. Shooting the wormhole—as their fearless captain put it—

sounded like going up the ass end of a centipede. In a sane moment, she'd politely decline. But there had been no going back since the launch when her body had been pressed so deeply into her chair that it felt like the skin was peeling off her bones. She couldn't imagine what the ERQ bridge experience would be. But she was braced for the unpleasant.

"You about done?"

Speaking of unpleasant… Dr. Harlan Johnson. Her lab roommate. Because although she'd traveled thousands of miles from Earth, he was still in her way. There were three labs on this ship. Barret and Rabiah took the lab that connected to the greenhouse on a lower level of the ship. Charles had multiple tanks of water in his lab, from fresh to brackish to saline. Not the environment her delicate equipment would appreciate, even with the sealed lids. So, through the luck of the draw, she was with Harlan.

She snapped the metal lock into place and checked the incubator settings again. "Just finished."

"Iver says we need to strap in. Everything needs to be secure. Came to do the final check."

"*I* can be trusted to follow directions." She wasn't the one with a problem with authority.

"What?" he said, as if he hadn't heard her.

Rather than pursue another verbal squabble, she inspected all her metal cabinets, ensuring they were latched and doubled checked that everything was tucked away or anchored to the lab counters. As expected, her things were as they should be.

Harlan picked up two pencils and a notebook from his station.

"Why do you insist on such antiquated documentation methods? Pencils are the tools of cheaters." She said the last part under her breath.

Harlan's mouth dropped open, but he turned away and secured the items in a locked drawer. "If we lose gravity, you're going to appreciate the usefulness of a tool that doesn't require gravity to work."

Leandra rolled her eyes. "If we lose gravity, my last worry will be how to write a note."

Lab data demanded ink. But there was no changing Harlan, and it was obvious why another scientist had so easily duped him.

One last check of the lab floor, including the open storage area at the far end, and she moved to the central corridor with Harlan too close behind. The ship was built like a beehive doughnut, with hexagonal cells around a central round tube between floors. The main level contained most of the labs and sleeping quarters. As she came around the corner, she found almost everyone else was already seated in the padded fold-out chairs with their chest straps securely in place. No one knew what to expect, so the protocol was similar to the launch standards. Everything and everyone locked in and braced for God only knew what.

Dr. Tengan gave each member of the group a clip-on dosimeter to wear.

Leandra didn't reach for hers. "I thought this ship had sufficient shielding to prevent radiation exposure."

"It does for known situations. But Iver pulled in all the solar array blankets so their cells aren't damaged during the crossing. We won't need them again until we reach another solar system. And since we're heading into the unknown..."

Leandra took the device and pinned it to the top of her shirt—one more thing to worry about.

The previous four ships may have made it through—or not. There was no way for them to communicate their success to the ships that had yet to cross. Team Japheth could be like a slice of lemmings. Solitary creatures gathered together unnaturally to follow each other over the cliff. Or into the ass of she worm in this case.

Barret raced around the angular corridor and dropped into the free seat next to Rabiah. Mahi tossed him a meter from her seat. He snatched it out of the air, clamped it to his clothes, and buckled himself in place.

Leandra clutched her straps as Iver announced imminent entry over the intercom. The launch hadn't scared her as much. Lots of people had rocketed into space for over a hundred years. They'd come back and gone on to lead long lives. But no one had reported back after crossing the bridge.

Harlan's hand settled over hers. "It's going to be okay."

A warm calm settled through her and only served to piss her off. Why would his touch steady her? "You don't know that. Don't give me platitudes. I have a right to be scared of the unknown."

He reared back, releasing her. "You do. Is it helping? Being scared and snapping at a small offer of comfort?"

She opened her mouth to speak, when a wave passed over her that felt like she'd passed through a funhouse mirror. Not in a reflection way, but in her body, being subjected to that undulating wave, stretching and distorting her and everything around her. Except that no one moved or changed or even shifted in their seats.

Then the rumbling started. She gripped the straps on her chair so tightly her knuckles went white. The ship was going to come apart around them. They would be lost in space, a cold death in the void. She opened her mouth to scream, but nothing came out.

Harlan wrapped his hand around hers again. She turned

her head and met his soft brown gaze. She didn't want to die with a man who hated her. But that wasn't hate in his eyes.

The rumbling stopped, and the ship jutted forward like a giant had flicked it out into space.

"Yes!" Iver's voice exploded over the intercom. "Everyone okay back there?"

"You all right?" Harlan's voice, soft and deep, blanketed her.

She nodded and forced her fingers to release, knocking his hand free. The others were disentangling themselves from their straps, chattering about what a wild ride that had been.

Charles whooped like a kid at a theme park. "We should go again."

Goddamn psychopath. Leandra clenched her jaw, holding back the scolding she'd like to give him about how much that sucked, and no, they weren't going to do that again. She had no idea if they'd have to do it again. But she sure as fuck hoped not. Being completely out of control wasn't something she'd sign up for willingly. Except that she had.

Harlan released the clasp on her harness and unclipped her dosimeter, his knuckles barely grazing her breast.

She slapped his hands away. "I've got it."

He raised his hands in a "don't shoot" gesture and turned away, dropping the meters with Mahi.

Shea paused next to Leandra as the rest of the team headed down the paneled hallway. "Cup of tea?"

"Yeah, I could use one."

"I'll meet you in the kitchen. Just need five minutes to start up my sim."

Leandra nodded and made her way slowly around the ship on wobbly legs. She settled into one of the eight metal chairs bolted to the ground around an oval table. Five minutes or five hours later, Shea was there, placing a lidded cup in front of her. Leandra wrapped her hands around it, soaking in the warmth. "Was that as rough for you as it was for me?"

"Yeah, felt like having your insides tossed in an industrial washer on the agitation setting." Shea grinned.

"How'd you recover so quickly?"

"I've always been a daredevil. Not as loud about it as Charles, but I love the adrenaline rush that comes with your stomach up in your throat. My mum hated that stuff, though, so I knew you needed tea. It fixes everything. Mostly."

Leandra took a tiny sip, and the hot liquid did seem to calm her. "Well, thank you. I'm sorry you had to take care of the wimp."

"Recognizing when you're in a life-or-death situation isn't wimpy. You're the smarter one. According to the data, adrenaline junkies are a lot more likely to experience injury or death."

Everything had shifted to a life-or-death proposition in Leandra's world. The realization felt heavy. She'd chosen it, so she couldn't even say she was uncomfortable, just weighed down. They finished their drinks in silence, and Leandra found the will to shake off the experience and get back to work. "Thanks, Shea. I'll see you for the evening meal."

"You got it."

Back in the lab, Harlan was already logged into his laptop. His long body curled over the keyboard, broad shoulders at his ears, focusing intently on the display. Leandra unlocked the incubator where her precious experimental cells were multiplying. She pulled one dish to check the progress and see if it was ready for freezing. Under the microscope, the image on the screen made her blink. Her throat tightened as the loss registered. It couldn't be.

The cells were dead.

She inspected the rest of the half-dozen trays. Dead.

All of them.

She swiped at an unprofessional tear that leaked out. "Did *you* do this?"

Harlan swiveled around to stare at her with a narrowed gaze. "Do what?"

Accusing him was a mistake. She had no proof. Besides, it was more likely that the transition through the bridge had caused the failure. She shouldn't have been in such a big rush to get started, but there was so much to do. And while it seemed like they had all the time in the universe, the goals of the mission were nearly impossible—a voyage across uncharted space to connect up with other ships, somehow build a space station, foster a multi-generational community, and find planets to terraform all before the originating teams died out.

She could wallow in her initial failure and the overwhelming nature of the project, or she could start over after doing a full analysis of what could have gone wrong besides the ERQ crossing.

"Never mind. Forget I said anything." Without proof, her accusation would be a repeat of her public attack but in close quarters. And if the man were capable of ruining her work for spite, what would he do to her when no one was looking?

Any tiny passing thought of getting involved with him romantically again died along with her cells. He was pretty to look at, even better-looking than when they were in college together and she'd been so infatuated with him to the point of pursuit. Going forward, she'd have to keep a closer eye on her work and him. He might be far more dangerous than she'd suspected when she'd uncovered the falsified data in his paper discrediting all the methods she'd used so successfully to help couples become parents.

Publishing bad data could lead to years of wasted experiments as others tried and failed to replicate the work or ran down false paths indicated by the publication. A waste, but not on the same level as the life-and-death situation they'd been in since leaving Earth. If he really was that unethical, they had much bigger issues than some dead cells.

CHAPTER 6

HARLAN RACED to the lab before the daytime lighting was at full strength in the corridor, desperate to start before anyone else was awake, especially Leandra. After weeks of recreating his processes that had been compromised, likely due to traversing the wormhole, he was anxious to see some progress. He slid his hand over the mouse to wake his machine. The gene mapping he'd started the night before had once again halted mid-mapping. No logical explanation existed. He'd been over the settings multiple times. From what he could tell, it stopped approximately thirty minutes after he'd left to get some rest, after hours of monitoring its progress, after Leandra had left the lab to sleep.

She'd been driving hard, fertilizing the eggs, growing her blastocysts in the incubator. He had no idea how much material she'd already appropriated, but if he didn't get his mappings done and start stage two—genetic editing—how could he prove that his theory was sound? Prove that his method, developed to increase the success of bringing back extinct species, could be applied to human fertility? Finally dispute everything she'd said about him in world-televised interviews with evidence.

Initially, he'd been fine blaming the failures on crossing

time and space so quickly. But there was no odd space event to blame this time or the previous one. He reviewed the setup again and checked the data in the logs. No error events. Everything just paused spontaneously again. There could be only one explanation—human intervention. But he and Leandra were the only people with access to their lab. An oily stab of dread shot through his gut.

She wouldn't...would she?

There had to be another explanation. Maybe the others were having issues too, although no one had brought up any problems at their semi-regular dinners together. He left the lab, too disgusted to start over a third time—at least not yet. In the kitchen, he found Rabiah brewing cups of coffee. "I'm going to be really sad when we run out of those little pods."

Rabiah turned. "Good morning, Harlan. Don't worry. One of my big priorities is growing tea in our greenhouse. Did you know that green tea is beneficial to your health and contains a reasonable amount of caffeine? But it's not like we don't have a ton of these pellets." She dropped the used grounds in the compost bin and loaded the next pellet. "It's kind of amazing how little space they take, flattened like they are. And no waste."

"So your plants are doing well so far?"

"I have the first starters, tomatoes and lettuce. I didn't bother to try anything until we were on the far side of the bridge. Too many unknowns."

"Smart."

"Barret had a little trouble with his larvae. Not completely unexpected, but still disappointing."

Harlan jumped on the detail. "Any progress since?"

"He decided to wait until my plants are established. He's got some ideas for getting a beehive started, but they'll need pollen, and the synthetic stuff has some drawbacks." She took the two lidded cups and moved toward the door. "It's not like we need to rush. This is a marathon, not a sprint."

"I need to make *some* progress. I didn't sign up for this mission just for the survival drills. But you're right." Except if Leandra was successful while he continued to struggle, he might as well shoot himself out of an airlock.

A slight smile lifted Rabiah's lips before she disappeared down the hall. Harlan retrieved a pressure-packed mini brick of coffee and made himself a cup. They were easily carrying supplies for three to five years, depending on consumption. And the freed space would allow for expansion of the greenhouse, but if Rabiah failed, they would be in deep water.

Maybe he should take a more relaxed approach, but gene mapping could be slow and the results time-consuming to analyze. And this was his last chance to prove to himself that his approach to fertility—something he'd cratered his entire career over—wasn't a waste. He'd never anticipated Leandra being on the ship when he accepted the mission, but if he could redeem himself in front of her, it wouldn't matter if no one else knew. Her having to acknowledge that he wasn't a charlatan, that he was an ethical scientist with groundbreaking, valuable techniques, would be worth more than everything he'd left behind on Earth. She'd killed his reputation. Only she could restore him completely. But first he had to overcome whatever was happening in his lab. Although, he was getting weary of reviewing, revising, and repeating his failed experiments. The lack of an obvious reason and the seemingly random nature of the failures had Harlan suspecting someone on the ship was sabotaging him.

"Hey, mate, why the long face?"

Harlan gave Charles a head bob and masked his spiraling concerns. "How's it going?"

"Great. Got my tanks set up. Ready to take some starter couples out of deep freeze and make some mollusk babies."

"So you're a fish pimp."

Charles chuckled and took his place at the brew unit. "It's a dirty job, and I'm just the guy for it."

Harlan reconstituted some soy-based scrambled egg substitute and sat down with his coffee.

Charles joined him with a protein bar. "How about you? Frankensteined anything cool yet?"

"Still mapping the genes. Had some hiccups with the bridge crossing. Any problems in your lab?"

"I heard that!" Iver stomped into the kitchen. "Ever since we got on this ship, it's been a total bitch fest about how the labs aren't set up right, this mechanical issue, that technical issue. They should have sent a team of technicians up with you coddled brainiacs." He punched the button on the brewer harder than necessary. "They should have selected some scientists who know how to use a screwdriver and a voltmeter. I get that no one likes getting their hands dirty and you all are more interested in saving the human genome, but what about saving your own asses?" Iver smacked a lid on his reusable cup and stormed out.

"Guess he's had a few complaints about the impact of the wormhole," Charles said to the empty doorway.

"Seems that way," Harland replied. "He's got a point. Mechanical failures to the ship are way more important than a lack of a perfect environment in the lab. Especially until we get to the rendezvous point."

"I'm not sure why he's so hot. I haven't complained. There's been some generalized grumbling about the challenges of working in space at dinner over the past few weeks. Nothing strong enough to warrant *that* reaction."

"Maybe Leandra or Shea?" Harlan asked. Most likely

Leandra. She could make anyone that pissed off with her holier-than-thou, know-it-all attitude. Although Leandra would be more likely to make a public scene, at least in his experience.

"Shea barely leaves her keyboard long enough to eat. I swear she's in the lab every time I pass by. She might be a vampire, mate. Any unexplained hickies?"

Harlan shook his head at the ridiculous comment. "Not yet, but I'll keep an eye out."

"You do that. I'm gonna head into the lab. Got some oysters I need to escort to the curb, get those bitches earning their keep."

"You're gonna offend the women with that kind of talk."

"Nah, they know I'm just joking. Besides, I'll blame you since you started it."

"Fair enough." Leandra couldn't really hate him more, so no big deal if she had another reason.

The question was, did she hate him enough to obstruct his work?

Back at the lab, he dug into the data stored on the server. Some of his mapping had been logged. Maybe he could restart from that point after he verified his process again and backed up the data he did get. Leandra still wasn't in, so he took a moment to check out her data and logs.

After opening a couple of files, he leaned in and dug deeper. If what he was seeing was accurate, she'd been redoing her processes as well. There seemed to be a lack of results. Several cell samples were discarded as compromised. He wasn't that familiar with her work. They'd never been in a lab together before, but the waste seemed out of character with her controlling style. What did it mean?

CHAPTER 7

LEANDRA SIPPED her herbal tea and prayed her raging headache would go away. The last time she'd felt this bad was the day after Harlan had ghosted her, and she'd tried to drink her sadness away with cheap wine. There was no alcohol on the ship, but she'd tossed and turned all night because of the failed experiments— what they could mean and how to adjust to overcome the possible sources of the disruptions. There were no clear answers. Rather than go into the lab and face the man who inhabited her nightmares, she wandered in the opposite direction toward the med lab.

"Hey, doc."

Mahi's amber gaze lasered into Leandra. "You feeling okay?"

"Headache. Do you have any aspirin?"

"Of course. Come sit down. Let's check a couple of things first." The doctor pulled some instruments out of drawers and cabinets.

"It's not a big deal. No need for a brain tumor scan."

"I'm sure you're right. But we're in space. So better to get some readings and check them against your baseline."

Leandra swallowed her sigh and sat in the chair. Mahi slid

an automated blood pressure device over her arm. Leandra rubbed her triceps after the evil squeezy thing finally let go. "You know, they've figured out how to traverse a quantum bridge, but they can't design an automated cuff that doesn't kill your arm."

"Any chance you're pregnant?"

"What?" Her entire body snapped to attention.

"Don't act so shocked. It's a reasonable question." Mahi slipped an oxygen sensor on Leandra's fingertip. "I've seen the way Harlan looks at you at dinner, and I could cut the sexual tension between you with a knife."

Mari was likely mistaking Harlan's desire to stab Leandra for sexual tension. "I'm not pregnant. Guaranteed. And when you're done with all the romance e-books you brought, you can loan some to me. I stupidly brought histories, biographies, and a few mystery thrillers. I could use a dose of smut."

Mahi laughed. "Well, when you fall into his bed, see me about some condoms if you prefer not to risk it."

The chances of pregnancy were rare, even without protection. The chance of falling into bed with Harlan again was even less. No matter how much tension there was between them. She couldn't help the way her body reacted to the man's presence, but her brain was in charge.

Mahi handed her two white tablets. "Probably some stress. I can give you some melatonin if you're not sleeping."

Leandra swallowed the pills with the last of her tea. "No need. At least not yet. Thanks, doc."

In the lab, Leandra found Harlan waiting for her. "You feeling okay? You look a bit pale."

"Just a headache. Doc gave me some aspirin. I'll be fine." She tried to sidestep him.

"We need to talk." He shifted in front of her only inches away.

"Yeah, about twelve years ago."

Harlan winced. "I guess I deserved that. But you could have called me before outing me in multiple news interviews. Worried someone would miss the fact I fucked up?"

"Your *paper* basically called me a hack. Your *ground-breaking research* was a complete fabrication and would've led couples to waste years chasing fertility dreams that would never be realized. My methods are well-documented and proven to work." He shouldn't have been invited to participate in the mission on that falsification alone.

"My research was valid. The efficacy was...embellished. Not by me. My co-author did that behind my back. But the processes were solid." Harlan shook his head. "Look, I don't want to fight with you. I wanted to ask for your help."

Leandra's mouth gaped before she could catch herself. She snapped her jaw shut and eyed Harlan for any sign of deception but found none. "With what?"

"I've been having some trouble getting my experiments started. I checked the database to see if I captured any data, and I happened to note that you've been repeating a lot of initial fertilization series. I'm sorry I snooped."

His confession along with his apology deflated her defensiveness. At some point, they would have to work together if they had any hope of meeting the challenges of the mission. And the odds of two unrelated pieces of equipment going haywire at the same time were slim. She resolved to treat him as an unknown new colleague as much as possible. "I wasn't sure what to attribute the failures to. You're having problems with the splicer?"

"Haven't gotten that far. It's dying in the middle of mapping, over and over again. I can't find the pattern. And I didn't want to tear into your data without your permission."

She was almost impressed with his respect and the way

he'd focused beyond himself, beyond his own work, when he investigated what was happening in the lab. Not to mention the fact that he had enough documentation to determine there was a real problem. "Let's look at the data together."

Harlan opened his mouth, and Leandra braced for another snarky comment about how she should have come to him about his paper. "Good idea."

His hand went to the small of her back as he pivoted to guide her to his workstation. Her knees went jelly soft. Okay, maybe not a completely unknown colleague.

He shifted the monitor, and she took a deep breath and focused on the display. It was easier once he quit touching her. After staring at the two databases and going back and forth, Leandra sat back. "Our experiments are halting at the same time. Different when looked at separately, but no matter when your mapping fails, my incubator has a power warning at the same time."

"Can't be a coincidence. And the times are all over the place too. I think that's what threw me. The mapping wasn't getting hung up at the same spot or after the same amount of time. I tried adjusting the buffer settings and anything else I could think of that might be overloading the system and causing it to halt."

Leandra nodded. "I thought my incubator was faulty. Or the wiring. Maybe something's wrong with the ship."

"I hope not, since we're all depending on it working if we're going to survive. But Iver did say he was getting complaints. Did you talk to him?"

"I told him I was having problems in the lab with the equipment and asked him to check on it when he had time. I think I pissed him off, but I wasn't trying to." The pilot was a damn hothead.

"I can talk to him. Maybe offer to help, so he'll explain what other problems there've been."

"In the meantime, I think we're going to have to monitor our work directly as much as possible. If you don't mind spending even more hours in the lab." Did she really just suggest they spend more time *together*? Yikes. Maybe that was a bad idea.

"As long as it won't bother you, I'm fine with it. I've been trying to give you your space since I know we don't have the best...ah..."

"History?" Leandra filled in. His presence in the lab was bothering her less and less—or maybe more and more in a different way.

"Sure. Let's call it that."

"We're grown-ups. This is bigger than any issues we've had in the past, and I'm willing to work together if you are." Besides, if she was wrong and it was his attempt at payback for pointing out his shady data, she'd be there to catch him in the act. If all the problems stopped, it would still be correlation, not causation. Either way, she'd get the embryos growing and be able to continue her work.

"Of course. I'll go talk to Iver now if you can stay here?"

Leandra nodded. If he had killed her cells, Harlan was putting on a convincing show. Blocked mappings weren't quite as devastating, but he'd have to be nuts to attack his own work just to fuck with her. He'd never seemed to be that kind of crazy. And he'd just proven that he wasn't that sloppy. Hopefully, she wasn't completely wrong about him and this wasn't a total setup. She really didn't know him that well. Other than how smart he was and how good he was in bed.

CHAPTER 8

Harlan climbed the short metal stairs that led from the main level to the bridge that jutted out from the main ship. He hadn't been up there since the initial tour done in spacesuits while the ship was still attached to the space station where it had been assembled. Star clusters, gaseous shapes, and distant galaxies filled the video displays that showed the space outside the ship without exposing the pilot to tremendous radiation through windows. "Is this really what it looks like?"

Iver spun in his chair. "Slightly enhanced, but only slightly. What brings you up here?"

"Just checking in." Harlan tested the waters. "Any word from the other ships that already crossed?"

"Just received a ping sent from Team Shem. They've been sending generic messages periodically as planned. I replied, but I'm not sure how long it will take to receive and reply. We'll know more about how far ahead they are once I get the answer."

"That's great news." A spark of excitement shot through Harlan. The mission had worked. At least two ships had made the crossing and were en route to the theoretical rendezvous. But they still had a problem on their ship. "You seemed a bit pissed off earlier. I'm not a total idiot when it comes to power distribution and tracking down wiring issues. Do you need a hand?"

"Your lab partner said she'd had some experiments fail because of power issues. Have you seen the same thing?"

Harlan nodded. "Something's going on. My mapper hasn't completed a successful pass yet. Who else has complained?"

"Rabiah came to me about the timers on her recirculation systems. I've run some system reports, but the power is being generated within spec. I found a few solar cells in our blankets that have failed, but nothing significant. I haven't had time to run down every wire in the ship. It's a brand-new ship. And Shea's been bitching from day one about her power needs for her quantum computers. If the bitching had started after the wormhole crossing, I might have more concerns about a system failure. But the logs look good, and we haven't had any obvious brownouts."

"Are the batteries working, holding the charge?" If the batteries failed or were drained, that could be a big issue.

"Based on the reports, yes. The thermo-gen is taking over as the main source, converting the heat as planned. But the solar cells are still feeding them, too, even at the reduced rate."

"Something has to be wrong."

"To be honest, I really don't want to crawl around for the next week checking every connection and outlet," Iver admitted.

"Is it all right if I check the wiring in my lab? I can let you know what I find out."

"Yeah, go for it. You'll need tools for panel access. I can get them to you. Bring them to the lab?"

"That works." Harlan pointed at the displays. "Wish we had some windows. I'd love to see this with my own eyes."

"Here, put this on." Iver handed him a dosimeter. As soon

as Harlan clipped it on, Iver pressed a button, and a large section of shielding slid back, exposing the vast space on the far side of the wormhole.

Harlan gasped. There were no words for how small and insignificant he felt before the vast beauty. The colors weren't quite as vivid as the displays, but his belief in God was cemented firmly by the experience. He nearly wept as the shield slid closed.

"Awe-inspiring, right?"

"I could stare at that forever."

"Forever would be very short if you left the shield open long. Wait a month or two, and I'll open it again for you."

Harlan slapped palms with Iver, nearly forgetting why he'd come to the man in the first place.

After dropping his meter with Mahi so she could add the readings to his health log, Harlan returned to his lab. Leandra was poised over a microscope, her thick braid drawing his gaze down her back to her still-perfect ass. His hands ached with the need to hold her against him again. Bare skin, heat, kisses all over her body... His cock reminded him for the hundredth time what it felt like to be inside her for that short, perfect moment they'd shared all those years ago.

She straightened but didn't turn. "Are you going to keep staring at my ass or tell me what Iver said?"

"Do I have to choose?" Shit. He should not have said that out loud.

She shook her head, her braid swinging. The urge to tug her to him—find out if her lips tasted the same—blasted over him. He stifled the ill-advised lust and came around the lab table to face her. "There have been multiple reports of power issues. Rabiah had some trouble with her timers. I'm planning to check the wiring for this lab to verify there are no loose connections or anything out of spec. But it's likely a ship problem."

"How is it a ship problem when it only happens when we aren't in the lab? It's too random and too predictable at the same time. And Rabiah mentioned those timers weeks ago at dinner. She hasn't mentioned anything since, and we're still having problems."

Harlan shrugged. She had a point, but he didn't have any answers. Except that it was unlikely that Leandra was doing something to disrupt him specifically.

"I'll talk to Rabiah while you trace the electrical." She cleaned up her workspace, tucking the delicate cells back into the incubator. "If we can't track down a physical cause, we need to consider there may be someone on this ship who doesn't want us to succeed."

It sounded paranoid, but he'd been willing to suspect Leandra. And the problems had only occurred when they weren't there to monitor the lab. A wiring problem wouldn't care who was watching. Was it that far a stretch to think it could be someone else on the team? But if it was—no, he couldn't go there. He'd find the problem with the electrical systems and fix it.

Leandra climbed down the ladder in the central tube to the lower deck. The greenhouse lab and all the supply storage filled the bottom level of the ship. Clear doors showed Rabiah hard at work arranging bags of soil, slicing them open, and inserting drip irrigation tubes and tiny sprouts. Leandra rapped her knuckles on the glass.

Rabiah peered up at Leandra and paused before waving her in.

Leandra took a deep breath of the humid air that smelled like Earth. A pang of homesickness squeezed her heart. "Sorry to bug you."

"No problem." Rabiah tucked another plant into the soil. "I'm just not used to anyone coming to visit. Do you mind if I keep working? I finally have some decent sprouts, and I want to get them in the dirt and under the larger grow lights so we might have fresh lettuce and tomatoes sometime this year."

"Of course. Can I help?"

"I'm fine. Kind of got a system. What brings you down here?"

"I heard through the grapevine you had some trouble with your systems?"

"I could not keep my recirculating drip system working. Iver seemed to think I was overreacting, but it's a delicate system. With every exhalation, you're expelling water and carbon dioxide. My plants need that. We gather all the excess from the ship through filtration units and funnel it down here. That water is critical to keeping everything growing, especially at the germination to seedling stage. One gap, and everything dies. They're hardier once I get the plants to a certain maturity, but at first..."

"I understand. It's the same for my little embryos."

"Even your waste is recycled for use."

Leandra could have done without that visual.

"And unlike you, who can harvest additional DNA from the team, no one is sprouting additional tomato seeds. If I kill all the seedlings, we're screwed for fresh food until we rendezvous."

"Have you seen any power issues while you're working?"

Rabiah paused, and her face shifted into a frown. "No. It always happens after I've left the lab."

"What about the bugs?"

"Barret has only recently restarted his work. The wormhole wasn't kind to his larvae."

"But if there are no bugs, the plants won't produce, right?"

"There are other methods." She half shrugged. "Not ideal and very time-consuming, but I could make it work in a grow space this size. First, the seedlings have to grow. This is my third batch and the only ones to make it to growing beds. I haven't begun to tackle the hydroponic system."

"The power outages stopped?"

"I assume Iver got off his throne on the bridge and fixed whatever was wrong."

"Thank goodness. I'm looking forward to tomatoes." And figuring out what changed for the greenhouse power setup.

"How are your babies coming along?"

"Not great. My power issues continue. I haven't been able to incubate viable embryos for cryo."

"There's always the old-fashioned way." Rabiah laughed. "That is why they picked younger scientists, right?"

"How long have you and Barret been married?"

"Since before grad school. When you know, you know." Rabiah ripped into another bag of dirt, slicing open the middle.

"I used to work with a lot of couples who had trouble conceiving. Did you ever consider—"

"Oh hell no. I'm child-free by choice. We both agreed to put our careers first. Barret's bugs are his babies. You should see the lengths that man went to trying to save certain species. And I much prefer the conversation of plants to pre-pubescent humans."

"How are you going to avoid conception? None of us are on

birth control. There're condoms on board, but those are probably limited in number."

"Tea."

"What?"

"Special herbal recipe handed down through the matriarchal line of my family. They have teas for everything—conception, fertility, and avoiding both. I can share. I brought plenty, and I plan to grow the herbs needed."

Leandra laughed. "I'm in no danger of that."

"You sure? I've seen the way hunky Harlan follows your every move. The man can't keep his eyes off you."

Leandra shook her head. He was probably just making sure she didn't stab him like Rabiah was stabbing the soil. "You know, I'd really like to try my hand at gardening with you sometime after you have everything going. It seems very therapeutic."

"It is." She stabbed another bag open and slapped it up on the shelf next to the other victims as Leandra showed herself out.

Odd that Rabiah had been the one to insist that she and her husband come on this mission when she seemed opposed to the very core of its existence—producing more humans. Both she and her husband were avoiding having children and didn't have anything to do with the perpetuation of the species beyond feeding the team. Even that wasn't an urgent requirement. The ship had plenty of freeze-dried nutrition. They would survive with or without tomatoes. And terraforming would be a long-term project, initiated by the teams who successfully rendezvoused but carried out by future generations.

Leandra rushed back to "hunky Harlan." Maybe he'd found the source of the power problem and she was just being paranoid when she allowed herself to believe someone was attacking the lab on purpose.

CHAPTER 9

Harlan tried to stifle a yawn. After ten days of practically living in the lab, the lack of good sleep was catching up with him.

"Take a break." Leandra lifted her gaze from the microscope. "I made us a rest area. Well, a padded spot to take turns sleeping." She swiped the back of her arm over her forehead, pushing tendrils of hair off her face and exposing the fatigue in her eyes.

"We could both use some rest. There haven't been any more failures." Not since they'd been manning the lab day and night, tag-teaming for meals, showers, and brief periods of sleep. Leandra hadn't left the lab for more than two hours at a stretch. He'd been just as resistant to leaving *her* alone in the lab. But she'd started to suffer from their self-imposed sentry duty—shoulders sagging, moving slower around the lab.

"Not yet. I'm so close to having another batch ready for cryo-preservation. I should have so many more done. I can't risk leaving the lab now."

Harlan stretched his shoulders, wincing at the tightness. "You're doing great. And, hey, I finished my first mapping today."

"I know. Once you do your splicing, we should look at using some of your modified eggs to create the next zygotes."

"I haven't decided what modifications would be the best to start with. Charles has some aquatics I can use. But you seemed opposed to planning for water-based planets." And the more time he spent with her, the more he was coming to trust her judgment and understand how she ran a successful business. She missed no detail, but he suspected it had more to do with a fear of failure than her natural state of being.

She yawned. "I really wish you'd found a wiring issue and we'd been able to maintain normal hours. I feel like my focus is fading and I'm going to miss something. I've gone over every bit of data we gathered from the failed experiments, but I still haven't found a pattern beyond the longer the task takes, the more likely it is to fail."

"We might never be able to explain it, but it's stopped now. We should be able to move forward."

"I'm fine with trying some mods with Charles's genetic samples. What did you have in mind?"

Harlan laid out two of the three possible options. Leandra yawned for the fifth time. Harlan couldn't hold back his own sympathetic response. "Let's pause for now. I'm dead on my feet, and so are you."

"We can't both leave the lab." Her voice was strained.

"You made a nest." He glanced at his watch. "Everyone else is probably asleep too. In the morning, I'll talk to Charles. See what material he can give us. Come on. I don't bite."

Unless she begged. He could be convinced if she asked nicely.

"Fine." She slid off the stool, and he followed her back to the pile of padding, pillows, and a thick blanket she'd tucked up against the wall between two storage areas.

"Lights on or off?"

"On," she said firmly.

Was that a comment on sharing a bed with him or fear that it might look like the lab was empty? At this point, he was too tired to care. He knelt beside her, pulled off his shoes, and spooned himself around her. "Hope you don't mind. It's kind of small."

She wiggled against him and pulled the blanket over her shoulder. "No funny business."

Harlan was damn far from laughing and trying desperately to control his desire. If she felt his cock against her ass, she'd probably kill him. As it was, the sexual frustration of spending so much time with her was making him wish he was dead.

She yawned. "Quit thinking."

He hooked his arm around her and pulled himself closer, hard-on be damned.

Heated weight draped across Harlan's chest. Leandra. Her leg was pressed between his, right up against his balls, and she was straddling his leg. The heat of her pussy was even warmer than her sweet, svelte body. He had one arm across her back, clutching her close. He ached to bring his other arm down, locking her in place, sliding his hand down to her ass. But that leg right up against his most sensitive spot kept him in check more than his own aversion to doing anything she didn't specifically ask for. One false move, and he'd be in serious pain. Not that he wasn't hurting with unfulfilled desire for her. He'd never quite gotten over her after college. And after so much time in the lab together, smelling her natural carnation scent, listening to her husky voice, brushing against her soft skin, desperation was taking hold.

She lifted her head from his chest. Her soft gaze locked on

to him. Harlan braced for her to bolt, but she shifted slightly upward and pressed her lips to his. He groaned and lowered his free arm to close the circle around her. Kissing her back, he deepened the connection. The hot, wet heat of her mouth, the teasing touch of her tongue, was even better than he remembered. He slid one hand down and ran the fingers of the other through her hair. She arched up, breaking their connection. A slight smile teased the corners of her lips, the scar tugging it slightly off-kilter. Her hand covered her mouth. Did she even realize she did that?

He gripped her fingers and brought them to his lips.

"I think we nearly had sex in our sleep." Leandra tapped his upper lip. "We should probably stop this right now, or I'm will need Rabiah's tea."

Harlan clung to the hint of desire in her voice. It was so rare for her to drop her shields and show any emotion, much less reflect any of his attraction for her. Attraction that only seemed to grow stronger each day they spent together. She seemed softer, easier, sweeter. He lifted his head to kiss her again, but she pressed her hand to his chest. "Morning breath."

"I assume mine. You taste sweet."

She shook her head.

"What's with the tea?" He disentangled their limbs and stood, offering a hand to help her up as well.

She stepped back and straightened her clothes and hair, avoiding his gaze. "It's a...contraceptive concoction. I mean, obviously I don't need it. I was just making a joke. I—"

Harlan pressed his lips to hers to stop her from continuing to defend herself. "You're right. You don't need it—yet. Or ever. Because if we get back to that point, I'm not letting you go again. I'm not that much of a saint."

"Oh. Um..."

"I'm going to shower and find some breakfast for us. You okay waiting here until I get back?"

"Uh-huh." She nodded, looking a bit disoriented.

He hesitated to leave her alone because their connection was so fragile. The urge to impress her, cleaning up and bringing her food, overrode his fear that she would second guess their tentative reconnection in the time he was gone. He'd have to hurry.

After a quick shower and a stop by the kitchen, Harlan returned to find Charles in the lab chatting with Leandra. Harlan passed her one of the coffees and a protein bar before turning to Charles. "How's everything in the water world?"

Charles chuckled. "Not as good as in baby-making land, but I did get some success with my mollusks. Working with some freshwater fish eggs today."

Leandra ran her fingers through her hair, pulling it forward. "Charles was asking about your mapping."

"Yeah, mate, Leandra said you finished a map finally."

"I did," Harlan answered. "I was actually going to ask you for some genetic material. I was thinking about adding enhanced lung function. Maybe even gills?"

"You're going for the big win. I was leaning toward making some evolutionary bumps." Charles shrugged. "Besides, if we're lucky enough to find a water-based planet, we should leave it alone based on humanity's track record with the oceans."

Leandra crossed her arms. "How can you two assume we'll find water, especially in any kind of composition that is compatible with aquatic life from Earth? We're better off considering planets with similar compositions to our home solar system and preparing for those."

"We don't know. But that's why we have years and generations to experiment." Charles grinned at Leandra, and Harlan tried to ignore that the man's surfer good looks might appeal to her. "I mean, really, we've got to birth and raise the next generation of human scientists while we figure out what planets are a possibility, and we still have years to travel before we hit the rendezvous point. Might as well have some fun while we're at it."

"More efficient oxygen extraction could help us with anaerobic atmospheres, and gills could be adapted for arid conditions to filter out dust or other debris in storm-prone environments," Harlan said, hoping to convince Leandra because the last thing he needed was another conflict with her. He wouldn't pursue the aquatic splicing if she wasn't on board. The entire crew hadn't had the opportunity to become a team because of the aborted training schedule. But they had to act like one if they were going to thrive or even survive. He could make several more arguments to support his position, but he kept his mouth shut and waited.

After a long pause, she said, "I could see that."

"Yeah, and since we have years, decades even, we can set the protocols for how these planets are to be treated. Set some limits on the destruction humans can do," Charles added.

Harlan was surprised how many team members were not pro-human. "If you think humans are the problem, and I'm not saying you're wrong, why would you join the project if you really don't want humanity to terraform these planets?"

"Because they were going to go with or without me. At least this way, I can have some influence on the impact and approach we take. Yes, we want humanity to go on, but how about in a more evolved, less destructive manner? We're the aliens in this scenario. Let's try not to kill the natives for once."

Fair point, but enough theory. "Has the power stabilized in your lab?"

"I took a page out of your book. I'm pretty much living there to keep an eye on everything. In fact, I should get back."

After Charles left, Leandra nudged Harlan. "Is there anyone on this ship who *is* pro-human procreation?"

"Well, I have to admit, I'm a fan of the procreation part. But I'm a zoo guy. Not sure I counted in the first place. Would it be tacky to say I'd love to help you make babies?" He was pushing it but had to see how she'd respond.

Her cheeks turned a beautiful shade of dusty pink. "I...um...came up with some time-boxed procedures for us to try so that maybe we can leave the lab occasionally."

"Sure. But I don't mind staying in the lab, especially if we get more nap time."

Leandra blinked and shook her head.

Harlan loved that he was effecting her, because she was absolutely affecting him.

"If we keep having power problems, we'll have to find out who's behind it. We've eliminated the wiring, and it's not random mechanical failure, because when we're in the lab, everything works. But we can't really live here. In fact, I need to take a shower." She picked up the protein bar and her coffee and retreated.

Harlan hated the idea that someone on the ship could be intentionally hacking their lab's power or coming into their lab to sabotage them. If he and Leandra were forced to publicly accuse someone of such a heinous action, they would have to be absolutely sure. He'd much rather spend his time seducing Leandra than tracking a corrupt co-worker. But as experience had taught him, doing the right thing often meant sacrificing happiness.

CHAPTER 10

Leandra took extra time after her shower to lotion her skin and brush her hair until it was dry. In those brief hours with Harlan, she'd had the best rest since she'd left Earth. Once again, one night wasn't enough. It didn't matter how long it had been since their one night together. She was still attracted to him, maybe even more so. And he was definitely flirting.

What had changed?

Was it just the proximity?

Workplace romance was a thing, often due to long hours spent together with a common goal. But they had so much history, which could only complicate such a delicate and often disastrous romantic entanglement. Besides, she'd never succumbed to an amorous co-worker before. But none of her previous co-workers had been Harlan. Nothing about their relationship was simple or obvious. Leandra shelved her concerns and hurried back to the lab.

Harlan turned and smiled as soon as she entered. "Come look at this."

Leandra swallowed the urge to ask him about his feelings for her and went to him. He took her hand and led her to his station. She glanced down at their entwined fingers. His darker skin contrasted and complemented hers. She pushed away the rightness of the moment. He probably wasn't even aware he'd done it.

"Charles sent over some eggs and an idea of where to do the splicing. If we replace in the sequences here…" He tapped the screen, his shoulder pressed to hers, as he continued explaining.

His scent, like cloves but with a hint of unlit tobacco, whispered over her. Danger. A warning to be heeded, or a reminder of how hard he had burned her? Or maybe how hot she still found him?

"What do you think?"

"It's risky, but we have to know." She lifted her gaze to his. Smoldering.

"What's the risk?" His voice had deepened noticeably. At least, parts of her sure noticed.

"I'm…I'm not sure." Leandra swallowed. She released his hand. "What if it doesn't work? What if it does, but it produces an unexpected or disappointing result?"

"Failure is just a chance to try again with more insight. You can't let fear hold you back from discovering something life-changing."

The heat in his gaze softened her. "Are we still talking about lung function?"

Harlan's low chuckle rumbled through her core, leaving trails of need behind. "Yes. And no."

Like someone had rolled back the clock, Leandra was falling right back into him. But she couldn't go forward with him—a new experiment—until she understood what had failed the first time, because that night they'd spent together had been perfect from her perspective. "Why did you do it?"

"Do what?" He closed the mapping file, saving the results. The spinner on the screen twisted like the quiet between them.

He clasped his hands together, his eyes never leaving her, in a picture of patience.

Damn. She'd have to spell it out or drop the discussion. Did he have any idea how difficult it was to form the words and confront him face to face? It was one thing to snipe at each other, tiny barbs with no emotional weight. But they'd moved past all that. If she didn't ask the question, there'd be no way she could let their attraction strengthen. She sucked in a breath. "Why did you ghost me after that night?"

"Come here." He threaded his fingers through hers and guided her to the nest she'd made. They sat side by side, thigh to thigh. He took a deep breath. "I've thought about how I could explain myself a million times. I owed you that much."

"Then. You should have told me then."

Harlan nodded. "That night was perfect. *Too* perfect. The kind of connection that ruins lives."

"Because it was too good?" She scoffed.

"Yes." Harland kissed her knuckles. "I wish I'd explained myself then."

"What could possibly explain—" She choked on the question as the past punched her in the gut.

"I was weeks away from leaving for grad school. You still had two semesters to complete your undergraduate. I was headed to the West Coast. You were applying to schools on the East."

"We could have found a way. It was improbable, but not impossible."

"If we'd spent any more time together—more than we already had—I wouldn't have been able to leave. Or you might have tried to follow me instead of your dreams. I couldn't let that—" He blew out a harsh breath. "I never expected going from friends to lovers—"

"To mean everything."

"Yeah." He rubbed his neck with his free hand. "I was convinced I had to avoid you completely. That I wouldn't be able to resist if I saw or talked to you. And when the semester ended in a couple of weeks, you would've broken my heart."

"Instead, you broke—" Her breath caught in her throat, and her eyes stung. "You broke mine." Lifting her chin, she blinked away the tears.

"I didn't come through unscathed." He brushed back a loose tendril of her hair, exposing the scar she was so self-conscious about.

"You should have talked to me before you disappeared. It wasn't solely your decision to make." She freed her hand from his and shifted her hair forward.

"I was twenty-two. I'd never been in love. I didn't know what it meant to have a relationship. But I'd seen what happened to my mom's career. I didn't ever want you to live in my shadow. And you know it happens. More so then. But still."

He wasn't wrong. Leandra had multiple friends who had left good jobs because their husband was transferred or recruited to a different part of the country. As strong and independent as most women were, they were still the ones to prioritize their families over themselves, no matter the cost. "I owe you an apology for not coming to you when I found the error in your paper." She sighed and crossed her arms. "I don't think I've ever gotten over being mad at you."

"You mean I haven't been changing your mind these last months?"

"Of course you have. That's why we can even have this conversation." She took a slow breath, trying to ease the weight in her chest. "Everything I've learned about you on this ship has made it clear how badly I handled the issue with your paper. I just couldn't understand how you could ignore me and leave after such an amazing connection."

"It was, but it was also seriously bad timing. I had to take control of the only variable still within my power—continuing the relationship. But I should never have made the decision for both of us."

"Kind of an asshole-man move." But she wasn't sure she would've been able to make the right decision, and he had a point about how much either of them could have lost by changing their plans.

"I've learned a lot since then."

"About sex? I'm not sure I can handle that." But she was completely ready to test that theory.

Harlan laughed, as she'd hoped. "I was going to say about being a team player and trusting other people. The good and the bad. It's always a risk, but it's better to default to trusting your partners."

"Too bad we find ourselves in a situation where one of our team members on this ship might not be trustworthy."

"Well then, maybe we should. Maybe we've got this situation all wrong again. And maybe..." He brushed her hair back and gripped her neck. "Maybe we should find out if we're still as good together as we were in college."

She tilted her face up to his, exposed but not fearful of his judgment. He'd seen her good, her bad, and her ugly.

His lips pressed to hers. Heat and command. His tongue slipped along her lower lip in a teasing invite, and he clutched her closer with his free arm around her waist. She opened for him, allowing him back inside when she'd intended to be closed off forever from him. His taste, his touch, so familiar and yet more than she remembered. They'd been so young, tentative, unsure. But there was nothing tentative about his kiss, the way he teased her tongue or pressed his chest to her breasts. He'd grown into a man who knew exactly what he wanted.

A river of desire rushed down her spine to pool in her core.

CHAPTER 11

HARLAN'S EMBRACE, his lips on hers, had transported Leandra back to her younger, naïve self. It was as if they'd never left that dorm room with the morning light teasing through the slats of the blinds.

He broke the kiss. "We should take this somewhere more private."

Had those been the same words he'd used at the party all those years ago? She couldn't remember. Was it possible to repeat history a decade later in a different galaxy? If she went, would he break her heart again? "What about the lab?"

What if this was a plot to get her away from the experiments so he could...what? That was dumb. He'd be with her the entire time.

"I'm nervous too." His deep voice did have a waver.

What about the way her body had changed? What if they weren't as good together as they remembered? What if she really was a lackluster lay like her two other lovers had led her to believe? She made herself meet his gaze. "You have to promise me something."

"Anything," he replied in a soft reverent tone.

"Be honest with me. If this turns out bad or isn't what you

want, just tell me, because it's not like we can ghost each other." She clutched her ribs to hold herself together. "I'd rather be disappointed than lied to."

"I'm more likely to fail you. It's not like I'm twenty-two anymore. My body has changed." He patted his stomach, as if he was carrying an extra ounce.

Leandra glanced down at her hips and thighs that were definitely more woman than girl.

"How about this?" He held out his hand and tugged her up as soon as she grasped it. "Will you agree to have the worst sex of your life with me?"

She gaped. "What?"

He gripped her hips and tugged her close. His erection pressed against her pelvis stealing her insecurities.

"Let's agree up front to do whatever feels good or right or piques our curiosity, knowing it will be awful. And if, for whatever miraculous reason, it isn't terrible, if it's something better than that, we can talk about it. If it is awful, then no harm, no foul. We chalk it up as a failed experiment. Which we can either attempt to improve on it or not."

"That's preposterous. You want to have terrible sex with me?" She snickered, her hand covering her mouth. It was her nerves making the noise.

He tugged her hand down. "No, I want to have uninhibited sex with you. Sex that doesn't bring all the baggage with it. Just us, right now. As we are in this moment. Not our college selves. Not our feuding scientist selves. Just Leandra and Harlan floating through space, determining if we can make the stars explode."

And he had made the stars explode for her the last time. But that was the past, and everything was different. Could she risk missing the chance to find something with him again? Even if the experience was different—almost certainly would be—it might still be spectacular. "Yes."

"Yes?"

"I agree to have the worst sex with you. No expectations, no comparisons, no inhibitions. Just royally awful sex." He cut off her words with the press of his lips.

When he released her, his dark, heated gaze set her on fire. He grinned, softening his features. "I promise to make it horrible for you."

"You're ridiculous." But she tugged him to the door.

They raced down the hallway and crossed the threshold into his room, which was filled with his masculine scent. The door closed, and Harlan pressed against the length of her back. With his lips on her neck, his whispered thank-you sent electric tingles down her spine, leaving her muscles and her mind completely relaxed but wanting and ready for whatever came next.

Harlan shifted her to face him so he could see her eyes. Leandra didn't have the ability to hide what she was thinking— it played across her face like a chyron. Kisses would soften her anxiety. He didn't hold back, releasing every hope and fear that had lived inside him since he'd agreed to join the NOAH project—to give up everything for the unknown. He shared his shock that she was on the project, assigned to his team, and giving him a second chance. He told her silently with his lips, tongue, and hands how grateful he was for a second chance.

She tilted away with a gasp. "Naked. Now."

She'd already been reduced to one-word commands. The memory of her gasping single syllables during the night they'd shared was tattooed on his brain. They would burst from her like bubbles when he was doing what she liked. Harlan tugged off his shirt and then reached for the buttons of Leandra's uniform. Slowly, he freed a single button. Leandra knocked his hands away and raced through the remaining fastenings.

"Now." She unclasped her bra.

Harlan didn't require further clarification, grasping her still-perfect breasts in his hands, lifting one and then the other to his mouth. Her fingertips glided up and down his shoulders. The soft sensation teased his cock without coming anywhere close. He moaned over her nipple, and she shuddered. Intent on completing her request for naked, he freed the button on her pants, followed by the zipper, still tonguing her taut nipple. She ran her fingers through his hair and tugged him closer. He nipped her tight bud, loving the squeak of pain as she relaxed her hold. Still a tug of war for control, the best kind of battle. He licked and kissed the tormented tit, soothing her.

"Harlan." She pushed his shoulders, and he took a stumbling step back. In a moment, her boots were off, and she slid her pants and panties down in one easy swoop. Stepping like a goddess from a fabric pool, a living dream. Her dark hair cascaded down her smooth golden skin. Another dark patch covered the apex of her legs. "Pants," she ordered.

He stripped in seconds, his cock bobbing a happy dance in the air. She reached for him. He captured her hand and stepped back. With his free hand, he stroked his length slowly, gaze locked to hers, imagining what it would be like to slip back inside her. He released her. "Touch your nipples. Tease them for me."

"Fuck," she whined. She cupped her breasts. Pinched the bronze buds between her fingertips.

A drop of precum eased the slide of his hand up and down his shaft. Leandra's eyes followed the motion as she tugged on her taut peaks for him. She shifted her hand lower, grazing the soft curls that covered her.

"Stop." He squeezed the head of his dick, holding back the near eruption at the thought of her fingering herself. "No touching that gorgeous pussy. It's all mine, at least for tonight. I have to make sure I show you a terrible time. Can't do that if you're pleasuring yourself."

"Please." She ran her hands up her neck into her hair, tilting her head back in a perfect pose of wanton need.

A pulse of need shot through balls. Clinging to the shreds of his control, he commanded, "Lie down."

She turned, her heart-shaped ass capturing his attention as she crossed the floor. He was right behind her when she flopped down. He didn't give her a moment to settle as he lowered to his knees, spread her legs, and lapped at the place he'd been dying to return to since the day he left. Her taste exploded across his tongue, sweet and savage. Starved, he nuzzled her clit while attempting to lick up every bit of her essence, too precious to waste a drop.

She called his name. He pressed his thumb to her bundle of nerves, giving in to her every demand. As she lost control, her legs tried to close, but he kept her in place as they rode out her ecstasy together. Her shaking and popping out words—*fuck, yes, please, more*—while he made sure to wring every drop of pleasure from her—for her—that he could.

Finally, she went boneless, and he cleaned her tenderly before moving to lie beside her on the mattress. His cock begged for more, but his brain was perfectly content to rest beside her for as long as she needed, as long as she was in his arms. She rolled toward him and caressed his cheek, her satisfied gaze locked on him. A soft, slightly slanted smile on her lips—the first she didn't try to suppress or hide. Was she starting to trust him?

"That wasn't terrible at all," she said with a hint of teasing in her tone.

"Let me know when you're ready for my next attempt. I'm sure I can make it awful if I try harder."

She gripped his cock, and he moaned. "I don't think harder is possible. The biggest problem I see is deciding between sucking you off or fucking you into the next star system."

Harlan's brain short-circuited trying to find the right answer. "Uh...?"

Leandra pushed his shoulder down and threw her leg over his hips. "I'll suck you back to life afterward."

Words ceased to exist as she slid her pussy over his cock. Too tight. She paused, lifted, and worked her way down again. Slowly stretching to take him inside. Each twitch, each silken embrace, reminded him what it was like to be in heaven. The warm wet caress of her, sheathing him inside her, pulling him slowly deeper, made him lose all sense of reality. Finally, her hips met his.

There was no place, no time, no experience that was better than Leandra naked, owning him.

Her breasts bounced, and she undulated her back and tilted her hips up and down his erection. He gripped her ass, not to control her movement, just to connect on one more dimension. Her skin was so soft, and her strong muscles flexed in his hands. Not one part of him wasn't connected to her— her rhythm, her warmth, her heartbeat. Even the air he breathed was scented with her desire, and still he craved more. She clenched him tighter. A coil of electricity formed at the base of his spine, and his balls pulled tight, ready to release. He fought the sensation, waiting. Nothing mattered but her pleasure. He tightened his thighs and dug his fingers into her ass as she slammed down, threw her head back, and screamed as her pussy exploded around his cock. Electricity rushed through his cock, and he came with a roar so loud the lights flickered.

Leandra collapsed onto his chest. "Not terrible."

He embraced her, preventing her from moving off his spent cock. "I'll try again to make it lousy for you. Soon."

She laughed.

The vibration rolled through him, leaving a trail of joy behind. Nothing could ruin this moment.

CHAPTER 12

Harlan sucked back the disappointment as Leandra closed the top button on her uniform, hiding the last bit of her silken skin. He'd tempted her to stay in bed and enjoy a morning session of terrible sex. But she'd shaken her head and locked herself in the bathroom—not even quickie shower sex was on the agenda.

"Ready?" She raised her eyebrows. "Or I can meet you at the lab."

"Give me five minutes, and we can go together." Harlan whipped back the sheet and ignored his erection, pleased that Leandra couldn't quite keep her eyes off him. He was sure she was checking out his ass when he slid the bathroom door closed. A two-minute icy-cold shower helped him focus on the mission. There'd be plenty of time to seduce his woman again. He'd apologize to her every day for ghosting her back in college if that's what it took. Eventually, she'd be in his bed every night. She'd likely resist if he pushed too hard and demanded that she move her things into his room. Maybe it felt too fast for her, even though it felt about fifteen years too late for him. Or maybe she had other concerns. Eventually, she'd share what she was thinking. Eventually, he'd get back what he'd lost.

Hopefully.

As promised, he was ready in record time. "Breakfast."

"Let's check the experiments on the way."

Harlan let her lead. He ached to hold her hand or wrap his arm around her waist. But she was all business, and he had to respect her professionalism. They each went to their stations. Harlan turned on the display where he'd left his gene mapping program running.

Frozen.

Nothing.

It had died hours into a run sometime the previous night.

Leandra stared at him over the microscope. "My replicating cells are dead. They were nearly ready for cryopreservation." She lifted the ruined sample as if she were going to hurl it across the room but instead placed it on the lab counter. "Now what? At least I know for sure it's not you doing this."

Harlan recoiled from the slap of her words. She'd actually thought it might be him? She'd slept with him while still carrying doubts about his honor, his honesty, and his commitment to the mission? The logical part of him resisted his overreaction, but his inner rebel screamed, *Fuck you, lady.*

Not rational and not helpful.

He blew out a rough breath and pushed aside the verbal slap she'd given him. "I had no doubts about your integrity. Not sure how you were able to sleep with me if you still had doubts about mine. But that's neither here nor there right now. We still have a problem to solve."

"That came out badly. And it wasn't conscious. I just..." Her cheeks pinkened. "Since it's confirmed that it's neither of us sabotaging our work, we still have a mystery to unravel."

"I'm going to shelve this conversation for now. I agree we have to figure out who's fucking with our lab. I'm just about ready to give you modified oocytes for your fertilization and incubation. We can't keep losing the embryos."

"I shouldn't be so attached to them, but they've always been like my babies. Someone is killing my babies." She glared at the incubator.

There would be plenty of time to fix his love life. They'd already waited this long, and at least they weren't enemies. It would take time to completely heal their connection and build a real relationship. One night of unbelievably good sex—two, actually—wasn't enough, especially after they'd had years of being at odds.

"What do we know?"

Leandra straightened her shoulders. "What about Charles? Do we know why an Australian is on the American team? Australia was slated to launch their own rockets."

"It hasn't come up. But he's obviously more interested in his fish than humans. Of course, a few team members fit that description of being more interested in their research than the mission." Harlan went back to the night before they left. "Barret told me he thought the project was a waste because humans only destroy planets."

"Shea didn't have much faith in the operation either. She accepted because the assignment allowed her to be her own boss, which I get. It's part of why I started my own fertility clinic."

"When was the first failure?"

"Right after we went through the bridge." Leandra shuddered. "I blamed that horrible crossing for the cell death. Barret was the last person to join the team and strap in before we crossed. Maybe he did something while no one was looking."

Harlan nodded. Would Barret actively ruin Leandra's work? How could he have done it so fast, leaving no trace? "The failures did start after the wormhole, but I checked the lab's wiring and verified the results with Captain Iver. He confirmed everything in the system reports shows normal ranges. Nothing changed."

"Rabiah said Barret's larvae had issues traveling through the bridge, too. And I would assume this was just a weird space thing, but both the incubator and your mapper are failing at the same time…"

Harlan glanced around the lab. The equipment was top-of-the-line, the latest and greatest. He wished he'd worked in labs with the budget they must have had for this mission. The failures made no sense. "Iver was pretty heated the other morning before I did the power check. There'd been a bunch of mechanical and technical complaints. I know you spoke to him. And he said Shea's been complaining about power for her computer simulations since we left the space station."

"I'm fairly certain Rabiah went to Iver about her recirculation timers."

Three out of four women had confronted Iver about the power. "Charles was having power issues. But he's living in his lab like us."

"What if he's lying and using that story to cover his tracks? How did he know we were living in our lab? Did you tell him?"

Harlan shook his head. "I haven't told anyone."

"Iver has the most access, but I don't see his motivation."

"I don't understand why *anyone* would do this." It was worse than the asshole who'd faked some of the data in Harlan's published paper, and it pissed him off.

"We need to dig a little deeper to figure out who could be behind this. It has to stop."

"I really hate the idea of not trusting our team, but you're right. I'll talk to the guys. See if I can get any insight. You take the women?"

"Sure. But we're back to living in the lab. We have to get

viable embryos soon, or this mission will never succeed. What if we never successfully create the next generation? We aren't the scientists who will establish the new colonies on the planets. It's the children, grandchildren, or even great-grandchildren. But only if we can move forward now."

Leandra was right. Dammit. Harlan swallowed his disappointment at not being in bed with her again for the foreseeable future. He'd already lost so much time with her—his own fault. But still, the faster they found the culprit and fixed this issue, the faster he could get Leandra to commit to a relationship with him. There would be no distracting her from the investigation.

Regret twisted his guts as she walked out of the lab without a kiss or even a wave goodbye.

CHAPTER 13

LEANDRA'S FOOTSTEPS echoed in the wide metal hallway. A slip of the tongue, and she'd revealed how many doubts she still had about Harlan. Doubts she'd deeply suppressed until she'd so inelegantly admitted them. He had a right to question her; too bad she had no answers. Their sexual attraction and compatibility remained off the charts, but she wasn't on the mission to mess around with Harlan. She was supposed to be creating the next evolution of humans who could survive on whatever planets they found. Not knowing what to do about their renewed sexual relationship left her itchy to decide something, anything, if only so that she was certain what was expected from her.

She paused at Shea's door, the only member of the team using their private quarters as their lab. Her knock went unanswered. She pressed the button to open it, but the message on the electronic display showed it was locked. Shea must be sleeping, despite the faint light that shown under the door. Leandra would come back later, after visiting Dr. Mahi Tengan.

The doctor kept to herself almost as much as Shea. Of course, what did Leandra expect when they confined so many introverts in a large metal ship and gave them the very best equipment to play with? But how did a medical doctor fill her days when the people on the ship were young and healthy? Time to inquire.

Mahi spun on her stool when Leandra entered the med lab. "Headache?"

"No. I'm doing fine, thanks. How's everything with you?"

The doctor tilted her head. "Fine. Why?"

Leandra searched for a reason to visit. "Did you ever get the data from our dosimeters after the bridge crossing? I was curious. Heavy radiation can impact fertility."

"Do you need a pregnancy test?" Mahi reached for a drawer to her left.

"I mean in general. Not mine specifically." Leandra swallowed. "Has anyone else requested a test?"

"Not yet. But they did load up this ship with some attractive men. Like your lab buddy, Harlan. Talk about tall, dark, and handsome."

And smart. And good in bed. And probably not someone Leandra should have started a fling with, especially if others on the ship were attracted to him.

"Pregnancy in low gravity can be a problem," Leandra reminded herself out loud. Along with losing focus on her work because of the hotter-than-stars sexual chemistry between Harlan and her. "The quantum gravity from the engines helps, but I'm not sure it would be enough to have a safe, natural fertilization and implantation."

"Then there's the question of how long our bodies and instincts would take to adapt to this lower gravity. All kinds of studies have been done on sexual positions that increase the likelihood of conception." Mahi grinned.

"Most of that is a myth. This position or that position or legs in the air afterward." Leandra kept a neutral tone, despite her disappointment that a doctor would buy into those old wives' tales.

"True, but they were disproven in natural gravity. Being in space changes the equation. Don't you think?"

Had the variables really changed? Harlan's original reason for leaving her—that their studies, their work, were too important to be disrupted by distractions—was still valid. "Does it? I think all the same pitfalls are still present. And we came from an environment that failed to support fertility. Leaving the planet doesn't change who we are at a cellular level."

"You might be right. But I still recommend doggy style to get those swimmers as close to goal as possible."

An image from the previous night, of Harlan holding her hips as he pounded into her from behind, flashed through Leandra's mind, heating her cheeks. "Yes, that's always a good one."

"Are you sure you're okay? You look a little flushed."

"I've been putting in long hours. I probably need more rest."

Mahi patted her shoulder. "Don't burn yourself out. And don't worry about the dosimeters. The ship worked as designed, and there was barely a measurable amount of rads from the crossing. Iver's the one I have to keep an eye on. The bridge is less shielded than the rest of the ship."

Leandra turned to leave but remembered her original reason for being there. "Have you had any odd power issues in this lab since we left the space station?"

Mahi's brow wrinkled. "Why?"

Leandra waved her hand. "Had a couple of glitches with my lab, so I thought I'd ask. I'm going to get some coffee. Want to join me?"

"Another time. I have some work here to finish up. But

thank you. And stop by if you change your mind about that test."

Leandra left before she confessed more than she intended.

Shea was seated at the round table in the kitchen, curled over a bowl of what appeared to be oatmeal and scooping it into her mouth at an alarming rate.

"Hello, Shea." Leandra spoke in a soft tone, like something used to keep from spooking a wild animal.

The computer engineer glanced up, spoon paused midair, and smiled. "Hey, Leandra. How're things?"

Up and down. No, that only brought Harlan to mind. "Some progress and some challenges. You?"

"Had a breakthrough last night. Finally got some simulations to complete. Of course, I stayed up all night. Thank the stars for instant coffee. I still need to analyze the results, but I think I have data that will give us a path forward for terraforming one of the planet environments we're most likely encounter."

"What's that?"

"Uninhabitable surface due to insufficient ozone layer. I had the computer calculate establishing below-ground cities, like the reverse of Chaco Canyon."

Supporting materials brought in from a distant site to build an elaborate city from dirt. "Build down instead of up."

Shea smiled. "You got it. Get some microbes, insects, and plants established topside that can tolerate the conditions and start transforming the soil. Well, it would be a long-term project, but for the first time, I have results that didn't fail completely."

"The simulations sound complex. I'm struggling to consider all the variables you're incorporating. Air composition, radiation, temperatures—"

"Exactly. That's why I needed my computers up and

running. And I can't wait until we dock with our sister ships. One of them has the transport pods. We'll finally be able to get real environmental data to feed the sims."

"And there will be more people to interact with than just our small group."

"Meh. I'm not really a people person. More of a night owl."

Up all night. She would know if the electrical problems were ship-wide. "Have you noticed any power issues?"

"No. Everything's running great." She spooned the last of her oatmeal out of the bowl. "Gonna grab another cup of Joe before I get back to it. You want one?"

"I'm good, thanks." Coffee would only disrupt the nap she had planned for later. Harlan didn't seem to need to sleep, but after two interactions, Leandra was stifling yawns. But before she could rest, she had to track down Rabiah.

The resident gardener was exactly where Leandra expected: the greenhouse lab. But Leandra paused behind a stack of soil bags when the tense tones of an argument reached her.

"I told you this was important to me. My studies were going nowhere back at—"

"—I came. To support you." Barret's tone wasn't at all supportive—angry and accusative was more like it. "But that doesn't mean I'm going to compromise my values. I don't have to be happy about the goal of—"

The damn recirculating fans kept blocking Leandra from overhearing their disagreement. Why couldn't they yell at each other like normal couples?

"—humans are what fucked up the Earth." Barret's voice rose. "Trying to perpetuate the genome or procreate is only guaranteeing future disasters. I'm not donating my insect DNA for their Frankenstein research."

"You have a god complex." Rabiah matched Barret's

volume. "You think your way is the only way. Not being able to compromise is what had you on the way out of the university. If you hadn't come with me, you'd be home alone, jobless. Instead, you lied to me and to the mission coordinators when you said you'd embrace the mission."

"I didn't lie, exactly. I told them what they wanted to hear so I could support your dream."

"It sounds so enlightened when you say it, but it means nothing if you don't actually 'support the dream' with your actions."

"I'm helping. I'm working on establishing the colony so your plants do well. I want to see your plants on distant planets."

Rabiah released a frustrated grunt. "That's only half the goal. There is no point in terraforming if we don't establish human-based lifeforms to grow the plants and eat the food. Besides, do you really want to see my plants growing if you let your larvae eat all my seedlings?"

"I told you, that's not what happened."

"You'll lie about anything. I can't trust you."

Footsteps moved toward Leandra. She tiptoed out the door before she got caught eavesdropping. She could understand Barret's resistance to compromise, which often led to mediocre results or even failures. The argument she overheard solidified one thing—she absolutely would have been the better choice to lead this team. And she had to stay focused on the mission instead of her attraction to Harlan, because too many members of the team were actively against the goal of furthering the human race.

CHAPTER 14

HARLAN SPUN on his stool as soon as the door opened. Leandra darted in with a furtive glance behind her.

"Everything okay?" He went to her but didn't hold out his arms, despite the impulse.

"Good." She played with her hair, pulling it forward then brushing it back before meeting his eyes. "I talked to Mahi and Shea. But Rabiah was having a...ah...*tense* conversation with her husband."

"Learn anything?"

"Shea's happy with her simulations. Mahi hasn't had any issues with her equipment. She did mention how hot you are and offered me a pregnancy test."

An image of pregnant Leandra came to mind, but he filed it away. Not the time to deal with that desire. "And the Rabiah-Barret argument?"

"I didn't say argument."

"Didn't have to." Harlan crossed his arms and waited.

"I only heard bits and pieces, and I didn't stay long. I shouldn't have eavesdropped." Leandra bit her lip.

Harlan let the silence linger.

"Rabiah accused Barret of letting his larvae eat her seedlings." The words rushed from her. "And he was in danger of losing his job at the university before he joined the project. I think Rabiah wanted to go on this mission without him. He also said he wouldn't share any of the DNA from his insects with our team."

"Interesting. I asked him for some bee genomes right after the bridge crossing. Just like I asked Charles. Barret didn't say no—although I haven't followed up because of all our lab issues—and Charles came through." Harlan hated where the conversation was going. If they were really living with someone who would actively harm their projects...

"If Barret would sabotage his wife's work, he probably wouldn't hesitate to block ours."

Leandra wasn't wrong. And there were no contingencies for a criminal on the team. If he did what Rabiah accused him of, ruining the food supply, then they were living with a monster.

"We need to split our lab time so we can monitor the lab around the clock. But we can't live in here. One of us needs to take the day shift and the other the night shift."

Harlan flinched. They would never see each other. "What about the way we did it before?"

Leandra's cheeks colored, and she drew her hair forward.

"Right. You still suspected me. Guess I'm officially off the list now." All the lists. Like not even on the booty call list. Damn, that stung. "Didn't think the sex was that horrible." He winked to take the heat out of his words but barreled on. "But yeah, the split days works." No point in allowing her to explain why she's good with not seeing him at all. Maybe that's why she mentioned Mahi being attracted to him. Easier to move along if he was otherwise occupied.

Unless he was overthinking everything. Setting aside the personal for the project would be within her character. Exactly what he'd done back in college, only she'd put him on the receiving end of the rejection. It was more than a little uncomfortable. Luckily, she couldn't exactly move across the country to ghost him.

"Why don't you take the lab for now." Harland sidled around her toward the door. "I'll grab some rest if possible and come back tonight to relieve you. We still have the nest, so until I get used to the new schedule, I'll stay up as late as I can and then crash here. Shouldn't take more than a couple of days."

"Harlan." Leandra's tone indicated she'd like to say something more, but he stepped back.

"I'll see you at shift change." He gave her a single nod and left before he broke down and begged. That would not be the way to win her heart, and his own needed a bit of protecting.

Harlan slept fitfully, off schedule, light seeping in from the hallway, and his mind racing with the possibility that someone on the ship could be actively attacking their work. He ached with the need to be back inside Leandra. Despite her distancing, he saw a future for them, raising the next generation of scientists, terraforming new planets, and enhancing humans to live under the conditions they found. When the alarm went off, relief flooded him. At least he'd see Leandra for a few minutes as they transferred the protection of the lab.

It turned out to be a *very few* minutes. She babbled about how the lab was fine and ducked her head as he tried to kiss her cheek. He got a mouthful of hair before she darted out the door. That had been hours ago, and he caught himself nodding off in front of his notebook. He erased the errant pencil line and went back to recording his findings. Moments later, the lab lights dimmed, but he couldn't be sure it wasn't his eyelids drooping again. After checking that his mapping was still running and

Leandra's incubator was still functioning, he made the call to rest for a couple of hours. First, a quick trip to the kitchen to refill his water bottle. The lab would be fine for a few minutes.

The hallway was dim, the common area lighting designed to support the team's circadian rhythms. The rhythm he was fighting in order to protect their lab. But from what? Or who? The kitchen light was bright, and he had to blink a few times to adjust.

"Barret. Didn't expect to see you here." Harlan recalled Leandra's report on the argument. "Everything okay?"

"I'm a night owl. And Rabiah tells me I snore. I try to let her drop off first." Barret chuckled with a self-deprecating tone. "How's everything in your world?"

"Making progress. Slow, but steady." Harlan didn't want to give the man satisfaction if he was the saboteur. "Any news on the mission?"

"Iver received a reply from Team Shem. He announced it at dinner."

Leandra hadn't mentioned it, but she'd likely skipped the meal to protect the lab. "That's great news."

"Yep. Mission seems to be right on track. Couple more years, and we'll be putting together a space station of human... missionaries, I guess?"

"Pretty exciting. The first pioneers in centuries."

"Or the latest colonizers to ruin a good thing." Barret laughed. "Forgive my dark humor. It's late." He waved as he left the kitchen, leaving Harlan with a prickling sense of unease at the back of his neck.

Water bottle refilled, Harlan paced down the hall. He passed the lab, compelled to check on Leandra. Everything was quiet, the door locked. He placed his hand on the metal panel, wishing he had the right to open it and crawl into bed with her again. But if she wanted him there, she would've invited him.

He retreated to the lab, where the mapper whirred quietly and the incubator hummed. He left a single light on and settled into the nest. An echo of Leandra's scent teased him with comfort and longing, but he willed himself to remain in the lab as promised and closed his eyes for a few hours of relief.

CHAPTER 15

Leandra clung to her cup of coffee as she paced down the wide metal hall toward the lab. The light was on in Charles's lab. It would only take a minute to check in. She pushed on the panel, and it slid open. "Hi, Charles."

"Leandra." He grinned up at her, his arms elbow-deep in a tank of water. "What brings you here?"

"Saw the light on. Thought I'd see how things are going."

"Come 'ere. I've got my first hybrids ready for the tank." He set a dish of tiny mollusks on the sandy floor of the aquarium before resecuring the lid.

"How exciting. So, no more lab problems?"

"I'm focusing on saltwater right now. Less susceptible to temperature changes over a short period." He wiped his hands and arms on a towel and gave her a quizzical look. "I've been updating Harlan on the progress."

Why hadn't Harlan shared Charles's progress with her? "He mentioned something about it. But I wanted to see for myself. I'll stop by again."

"Sure, anytime." Charles looked as confused as Leandra felt. He hadn't confirmed there were lab problems or even that there weren't. And somehow, she'd disclosed that she wasn't talking to Harlan much.

She pulled a loose lock of hair forward and mumbled parting platitudes as she left. It was past time to get to the lab. After all, she'd made a point to set her alarm an hour earlier than she had the past few days. Although not really a morning person, she missed Harlan. They'd barely spoken since she'd insisted on split shifts. But she couldn't fight the compulsion to check on all the labs first. She hadn't spoken to anyone since she and Harlan had divided their schedule, too afraid to leave the lab unattended. A few more minutes wouldn't hurt. Circling back, she descended to the lower level and Rabiah's lab.

The grow lights illuminated tiny shoots, but other than the plants, the lab was empty. She returned to the main level at the opposite end of the lab, passing the medical office. A loud grunt followed by a high-pitched squeal made her pause, hand lifted to the door. Could Harlan have taken her off-hand comment about Mahi as a reason to have sex with her?

If she knocked on the door and Harlan was inside, she wasn't sure what she would do. It would be worse than when he'd left her in college, and there would be nowhere to hide to nurse her shattered heart. And if he was with Mahi, the lab was exposed. She raced away, letting her anger and betrayal flow through her. With a slap, she opened the door and froze. "You're here."

Harlan spun on his stool, forehead furrowed. "Where else would I be?"

"I, uh...I came in early to talk—" Suddenly in the dark, she froze. The lab machines clicked off. Above the door she'd come through, a small red light flashed on. Power failure.

"Shit!"

Leandra winced at Harlan's angry shout but was too afraid to move in any direction. A warm hand encircled hers.

"Come on. Let's find Iver and get a system check now while it's happening." Harlan led her to the hallway that was still perfectly lit. So the power issue was isolated to their lab? She freed her hand and tried to keep up with his long, angry strides.

As they passed Charles's lab, he burst out of a dark room. "I can't work like this. The power is off to all my tank heaters. Minor flickers are one thing, but this is a full-on outage. How long before this impacts *our* life support?"

Harlan paused. "I know, mate. Headed to the bridge now."

"Better you go. I'm likely to punch Iver if he insists there's nothing wrong again." Charles walked away in the opposite direction.

They neared the med lab, located just before the entrance to the bridge. Iver stumbled out, tucking in his shirt, his hair askew. Leandra caught a glimpse of Mahi wrapped in an exam robe, looking just as disheveled. So the comment about Harlan had been a tease? An attempt to get Leandra to confess to their relationship? Given that Mahi was intimate with Iver, the comment about Harlan's good looks made no sense.

"Iver." Harlan blocked the pilot's path. "We've got a problem."

"What now?" Iver huffed.

"Power is completely out in both Charles's lab and ours. Has been for several minutes. You can't tell me the systems aren't reporting any issues."

Iver ran his hand over his hair, taming some of the wilder bits. "There haven't been any alarms."

"Then we need a full manual check. Charles pointed out this could impact our life-support systems. The power issues are getting worse, not better."

"Let's check the logs first." Iver moved toward the bridge. "A manual check of every wire in this beast could take days."

"I'll help."

"I'll check the logs with Iver," Leandra insisted. "Your shift is over anyway, and you need your rest." And maybe Iver needed a second set of eyes. Ones that didn't miss errors in the data.

CHAPTER 16

Harlan stomped back to the lab, barely able to contain his frustration with the mission, the power issues, and Leandra. She'd dismissed him as if he were a child or her employee. He'd thought they were lovers, getting back to the space he should never have left all those years ago, even though it had been the best choice at the time. What a fool. She had no intention of becoming his true partner, didn't even see that he could be.

He walked past their still-darkened lab, staring at the doorway, and ran right into Barret.

"Whoa. You okay, Harlan?" Barret grabbed on to Harlan's elbows.

"Sorry." Harlan freed himself from Barret's grip. "Distracted."

"Women will do that to you. How about a beverage?"

"If you say you have a bottle of whiskey, I could be your best friend right now."

Barret snorted. "I wish. But it would be gone already. Rabiah's been driving me crazy." He led the way to the kitchen. "Somehow, everything that goes wrong with her plants is my fault."

"As if we need to do anything on this ship to have everything go to hell."

"Right? It's like the mission has been doomed from the start. Probably should've been."

Harlan wasn't sure of anything anymore. In the kitchen, Barret reconstituted some juice and handed a glass to Harlan.

"You know—" Harlan held the glass up to the light "—if we set this up under the right conditions, we could get it to ferment."

"That bad?"

"I've had so many setbacks, I'm getting to the point that I don't care about the outcome. And the prospect of life in this ship, or a collection of ships, feels like I've sentenced myself to prison." Harlan waved his hand around at the walls of the kitchen.

"I couldn't let Rabiah go on her own, but I wonder if that's what she actually wanted all along." Barret sighed and stared into the bottom of his glass.

"Give Leandra enough power to get through her incubation phase, and she'll have more than enough embryos to create the next generation. They don't even need us."

"Pretty sure women have always known that part. But I sort of counted on her wanting me."

"True." Harlan sipped his juice as if he could taste it over the bitter disappointment of losing Leandra. "What do you think's going on with the ship? I assume you've had power issues too?"

"I think God—or the goddess, or the universe, or whatever higher power you believe in—is done with humans. We've been chalked up to a mistake, and this last Hail Mary bullshit isn't going to be allowed to stand."

It was the strongest tone of voice Barret had ever used in Harlan's presence. And he couldn't disagree. Humans had fucked up. It appeared they still were—at least someone on the team was—unless God really was flicking their little marble around space, pushing them to fail. "You may have a point. Humans probably do deserve to go extinct. Guess I just hoped a new start, a smarter approach, was possible."

"It's still possible, I guess." Barret set his empty cup on the table. "We have two years before we rendezvous. And we heard from one of the ships. That's promising."

Harlan scrubbed a hand down his face. This wasn't him. He didn't think God hated him or the universe was done with humans. This was lack of sleep, lack of progress, and lack of Leandra's trust.

"Looking at the bright side, Rabiah can't throw me out, so I have two years to fix our relationship. At least."

Harlan refrained from sharing that years passing didn't fix anything if you didn't take action.

Barret stood. "Get some sleep. You look like shit."

"Thanks." Harlan tried to find the motivation to make it back to his quarters, but nothing seemed to matter. Not fixing the power to the labs, connecting with the other ships, or even the terraforming that came next. It all seemed pointless.

A shrill alarm sliced through him. The ship plunged into total darkness. A single red light shone above the door. Harlan froze. His blood pounded in his ears.

Life-support systems had crashed.

"*Emergency. This is not a drill.*" Iver's prerecorded voice clanged through the ship. "All personnel, take life-preserving measures."

Fuck.

Where was Leandra?

Had she been electrocuted?

Was she even still alive?

He had to get to her.

Training kicked in. First, get his survival suit on.

Harlan prayed that Iver would get Leandra to her suit. He raced to his room using the red glowing emergency lighting in the floor as a guide. They had three minutes. Their environmental suits provided just seventy-two hours of oxygen.

As he reached his open door, his stomach slammed into his throat. His feet left the floor.

Gravity was gone.

CHAPTER 17

"Wʜᴀᴛ's ʜᴀᴘᴘᴇɴɪɴɢ?" Leandra gripped Iver's shoulder, the alarm breaking her eardrums.

"Life-support failure." Iver tugged a package from under his pilot's chair. His survival suit. "Where's yours?"

"In the lab." Leandra sped down the stairwell back to the main hallway. Three minutes. That's what they'd told her in training. She prayed they'd underestimated that time. Would she remember how to put it on? To make sure all the seals and connections were tight? Why hadn't Iver scheduled more training? She could have practiced on her own, but she'd been focused on her lab, not her life.

The eerie red glow in the corridor didn't help her nerves. She kept her hand on the left wall as she jogged. If she went any faster, she'd likely trip in the dark. Better to maintain control. Walk, don't run. Wasn't that what people always yelled in an emergency? The labs that had seemed so compact stretched on. Charles's lab—only a few more meters. She brushed the frame of the doorway and suddenly lost her footing. Her stomach flipped. The free tendrils of her hair floated across her field of view.

No.

Gravity had failed.

Leandra free floated in the hall. She scrambled for a hand-hold. There was nothing—no way to control her momentum. No way to make it to her survival gear. She shivered. The air was noticeably colder, and she couldn't think clearly.

Where was Harlan?

Did he get to his suit?

If only she could see him once more.

She shouldn't have pushed him away. They could survive this together. He would've helped her. But she'd let her insecurities and need for absolute control become a wedge between them.

Tears pricked her eyes. Her head bounced off the ceiling, and she saw stars along with a bright light. Was she already dead?

A light swept side to side. Someone in a survival suit came up the hall.

Would they look up?

Would they see her?

Fuck, she was panicking. In a moment of clarity, she pushed off the ceiling and crashed into the only person who could help her. Harlan's warm brown gaze stared at her through his thick face shield. It was the last thing she saw before she passed out.

Leandra blinked her eyes. Everything was fuzzy. She reached up to wipe them, but her hand was gloved and blocked by—her helmet. *That's* why her focus was off. Where was everyone? Where was Harlan? He must have put her in the suit, but then he left her? There was no way to call out to him. The communication devices in the suits only worked in close proximity. She tried to stand, but a webbed tether held her in place.

She pressed her boots to the metal floor, and the magnets in the heel and toe locked on. Her carabiner released easily, the dexterity training finally making sense. A red light glowed over the doorway providing scant illumination but enough to determine that she was in their lab. It took a few steps to recall the right method of tipping her ankle to release and connect her boots.

A piece of paper was taped to the door. Written in pencil. Of course. For the first time since the power went out, Leandra smiled. Even under the light, she could barely read the words through her helmet.

With Iver. Back ASAP. H

Should she stay in the lab? Or try to help Harlan? How long had he been gone? As soon as she opened the door, a flashlight blinded her.

She held up her arm and waited for whoever it was to reach her.

Barret.

He offered her another flashlight. His voice came through her helmet. "Harlan sent me to check on you."

Shea appeared from around the corner, stomp-clicking her way toward them. "What the hell is going on? My run is totally fucked. I'm going to have to start over."

Barret gaped at Shea.

"Are you kidding me?" Leandra barked at the insensitive woman. "We're going to die in a matter of days if we can't fix this problem, and you're worried about a run? How about you worry about the oxygen levels or the lack of heat? Run any simulations on that?"

"I...I'm sure—"

"No. You're not sure of anything. None of us are. Welcome to the club. We've all been struggling to make things work. My work has been ruined and interrupted since we left the space station. The electrical systems on this ship have been a problem from day one, but would anyone listen to me?"

Before she said something she would truly regret, Leandra marched off toward the bridge. She circled the corridor, but Harlan and Iver were nowhere to be found. Harlan wasn't in his quarters.

A chill that had nothing to do with the actual temperature iced the blood in her veins. She was alone in space, about to die. Maybe not this minute or this hour, but the longer they went without basic support systems, the less likely it was that they could bring them back online. The interior wiring was shielded but still depended on a reasonable temperature. The computers maintaining the systems were likely even more delicate, no matter how ruggedized the manufacturers claimed they were. The limits were tested at the extremes of Earth, not space, and not ERQ bridge crossings.

She slowly made her way back to her quarters. There was nothing a fertility expert could do to improve their situation, so she might as well stay out of the way and conserve what resources her suit had left.

As she gripped the bed and clicked a tether into place so she wouldn't float around, two possibilities presented themselves. Either the ship's electrical problems had existed from day one and they'd finally reached the tipping point. Or the saboteur was willing to sacrifice their own life to prevent the mission from proceeding. But that only made sense if it was an organized effort and all the ships were carrying a traitor. Hard to believe a small, coordinated group could doom the future of the human race.

Or was it? Hadn't that been what had happened on Earth? Most likely unintentionally or, worse, with the best of intentions.

Did it even matter?

She closed her eyes. Of course it did. Everything their team and the other teams did mattered. She couldn't give Harlan a hand with the problem directly, but she could have faith and trust him to identify the failure while she reconsidered everything that had occurred on the ship. Because if they didn't identify and resolve the root cause, the mission was doomed.

CHAPTER 18

Harlan fought his way up the ladder instead of using his weightlessness to his advantage like he'd been trained. After seeing Leandra bounce off the bulkhead, he didn't plan to float anywhere. Once on the main floor, he clicked his boots to the hallway, still in the dark except for the eerie emergency glow. Fuck. He'd left her in the lab, unconscious but breathing. It was a shit thing to leave Leandra alone like that, but it had been the safest place. The magnetic boots made it impossible to move any faster as he attempted to return to her.

Gone.

Leandra wasn't where he'd left her. His note remained on the door. The tether he'd used to anchor her into their nest floated loose. A shot of adrenaline pulsed through him. Had someone gotten to her? The reaction was insane. No one had a reason to harm anyone else. The complete crash of the electrical system had left him paranoid. The only thing that mattered was finding her and making sure she was okay. He stomped toward her quarters.

The tension in his shoulders released. She was there, attached to her bed. But she shouldn't be sleeping after a head injury. He shook her, relieved when her eyes opened.

"You're here." Her voice filled the space in his helmet.

"Took a minute to find you. Why'd you leave the lab?"

"To find *you*. But I ran into Barret and Shea."

"Didn't you get my note?"

"I did—in pencil." She shook her head.

"Too bad I didn't plan beyond writing a note in an emergency."

"But you put me in my suit?"

"Only after you hit your head." If only he could touch her skin, check her head, her pupils. Kiss her. Run his fingers through her hair and hold her close. "You shouldn't be sleeping. You could have a concussion."

"Did Iver find the problem?"

"Not yet. I cleared the wiring in the lower level."

"Did you see Rabiah? I saw Barret and Shea. But I don't know if Rabiah, Mahi, or Charles made it into their survival gear." She freed her tether. "We should check on them."

"Charles helped me get you suited up. Where did you see Barret and Shea?"

"Outside our lab. Barret gave me a flashlight. Shea was complaining about her runs."

"All that woman ever does is complain, I swear." Harlan sighed. The one person not dealing with living organisms was doing the most bitching. A niggle of concern crept up his neck. "Have you ever been in her lab?"

"No. I've been everywhere else."

"She's been complaining about computing power and power in general since before we left the space station."

"Oh, shit." Leandra stood, her boots locking to the floor. "Let's go."

Harlan clung to Leandra, their flashlights filling the red glowing metal corridor with an eerie white light. Shea's quarters were on the opposite side of the circular hallway.

The open doorway framed a picture of chaos. Harlan swung his light from side to side, counting the computers that arced around the bed, forming a wall. Keyboards, USB drives, and other pieces of hardware not locked down littered the space. Wires extended from the ceiling and floated over the floor, leaving no path to walk.

"What the..." Leandra's tone captured the horrific truth.

Shea had overloaded the ship's power grid. Whether she'd done it on purpose or through selfish oblivion didn't really matter since they were trapped in space with no life support.

Harlan tiptoed in, trying to maintain his link to the metal floor. His left boot missed the connection, and he grabbed one of the computers. Warmth traveled through his glove. The computers must have been generating tremendous heat to still be warm enough to penetrate his suit after all this time.

"What the fuck has she been doing?" Leandra finally blurted out.

Overhead lights blinked on, momentarily blinding Harlan as his eyes adjusted. A cascade of beeps came from the metal boxes. Horror at the cycle that could cascade again if the computers rebooted had him tugging power cords as fast as he could grab them. Leandra freed the last two.

"What is that?" Leandra stared at the floor, the leg of her suit pressed against her, rippling. "Do we have a breach in the hull?"

Harlan leaped over the cords and held a gloved hand over the area. A rush of cold air. "No, it would be sucking us out, not pushing air in. I think she modified the cooling system to accommodate all these computers. They were generating a ton of heat."

Leandra freed her helmet and yanked off her gloves. Harlan followed her lead after she didn't turn blue from lack of air.

"This is what broke our experiments and killed the life support, isn't it?" she asked him. The dismay in her tone was evident.

"I think so." Harlan tugged Leandra into his arms when she shivered. Ice coursed through his veins too, not from the air but from the thought he could have lost this moment with Leandra. Lost his lifetime with her. Fuck the mission. The woman in his embrace was everything. He lifted her chin, intent on kissing her.

"What are you doing?" Shea's voice shrieked between them, and he twisted to look at the doorway.

CHAPTER 19

LEANDRA GAPED at the woman with the audacity to accuse them of something nefarious. "We're finally solving the mystery of how all our experiments were corrupted and how a team of scientists was nearly killed by the selfish demands of one of their members."

"Where did you get all this equipment?" Harlan glowered at Shea.

Thank goodness he wasn't directing that scowl at Leandra. The man was fierce when he was pissed.

"I was issued most of it with the mission." Shea hugged herself, her back rounded. Not quite the picture of justified entitlement her voice tried to convey.

"And the rest?"

Harlan's disappointed dad voice was kind of sexy. Leandra felt sorry for their future kids.

What? She did not just imagine having children with Harlan. Did she?

"I brought some of it with me. Some were underutilized, so I repurposed them." Shea's voice got softer as she continued to speak. Likely, as she heard herself, she recognized what she'd done.

"You took computers that didn't belong to you. Siphoned off the electricity out of the labs. And redirected the cooling systems. Never once mentioning it during dinner or any of our conversations?" Leandra held up her hand when Shea opened her mouth to respond. "No. There's no excuse. You knew what you were doing was wrong, or you wouldn't have been so stealthy about it."

Barret and Iver barreled into the room.

"You! You did this? Put all of our lives in jeopardy?" Barret screamed at Shea. "All of this. It all comes down. Now."

Barret's face was beet red, and even when he'd argued with Rabiah, Leandra had never heard him so loud or so enraged. He was beyond livid.

Iver placed a hand on Barret's shoulder. "Let's take a breath. We're all alive. The systems are running, and we can undo this mess. Nobody died, so it's fixable."

"You're on a disciplinary plan." Barret pointed a finger at Shea. "All of this equipment is being moved out of here. You're done."

Shea opened her mouth, but Leandra placed her hand on Shea's forearm. "You messed up."

"There are disciplinary procedures for the team," Iver reminded them. "We'll follow those. But Barret's the team lead, and he's right. You put us all at risk."

Shea dropped her head. "I'm sorry. I get...obsessive when trying to solve problems. I only planned to siphon off a little bit of the unused energy when the labs were dark. Run a few extra computers to get additional data. I didn't realize... I'll do whatever it takes to regain your trust."

"Shea's work is too important to stop," Harlan said calmly. "My suggestion is that we set up a reasonable amount of equipment in our lab. We have the space. She can document her planned simulations and estimated run times. The team can review the plans and help manage the compulsion for more answers faster."

His solution was perfect since they wouldn't need their nest any longer.

Barret ran his hands through his hair, leaving it standing on end, a literal mad scientist. Leandra stifled her inappropriate snort. He pointed at Shea. "Six months. All of your runs will be approved. And yes, you're moving the *issued* equipment into the lab with Dr. Richards and Dr. Johnson."

Barret hadn't used her title in months. He was really pissed, but his voice was under control. There was no risk of violence or overreaction. Not that it would be possible to overreact to Shea nearly killing the entire team.

Shea wiped a single tear. "I'm so sorry. I'll follow whatever plan—the six months...or longer. Moving to their lab. All of it. I never should have gone behind everyone's back and put the team at risk. The uniqueness of the problem, the quest for answers... It was like a drug to me to consider all the possible environmental variables and—" Shea took a breath, the first since she'd started rambling. "In the past, my enthusiasm and dedication have led to incredible breakthroughs. I didn't consider how hard I was stressing our systems."

"Since Harlan and Leandra will be sharing lab space, I'm happy to review Shea's simulations," Charles offered from the doorway. Rabiah stood next to him. "Make sure the passion for answers doesn't get out of hand again."

Shea blushed and nodded.

"I could be wrong," Harlan added, "but I'm pretty sure the personnel policies call for a ninety-day review of any disciplinary action."

"I don't mind working with Charles on my simulations. Or sharing your lab. It's probably best if I just agree to stick to that plan."

"Great." Harlan clapped. "Now, I'm taking Leandra to see Mahi. She may have a concussion from hitting her head during the loss of gravity."

Before anyone could reply, Harlan marched over, took Leandra's hand, and click-marched her in their magnetic boots toward medical. "You're moving in with me."

Leandra bit back her argument. Commanding Harlan was kind of hot. "Am I? Why would I do that?"

"Because with Shea in the lab, we won't have our nest. And we don't need it. But I need you in my bed and in my life because you're already in my heart."

The shock of his words pulsed through her heart, which hadn't beat quite this hard since she'd been with him the first time and fallen completely in love. She'd locked it away for so long, the sensation was foreign but with an echo of the familiar at the same time.

He moved in front of her. "I could get on my knees and beg. Might be kind of challenging in these damn boots. But I'll do it."

She cupped his cheek and melted into his eyes. "You don't have to beg. You're in my heart too."

He pressed a heated kiss to her lips. She tangled her tongue with his, caressing his shoulders, his muscular arms, pressing herself against his hard chest. His thick cock was captured against her belly. Fuck, she wanted him inside her.

"Thought you were *visiting* the doctor, not *playing* doctor, mate." Charles's teasing voice broke them apart.

"You're just jealous," Harlan said with a smug tone as he tugged her toward the med lab. In a low tone, he told her, "Good thing he interrupted. I might not have waited to get you back to our quarters."

Our.

CHAPTER 20

Harlan held his survival suit over one arm and clasped Leandra's free hand. Mahi had cleared her of any signs of concussion. "Let's drop the suits at the lab."

"We should stay. Get some work started. We're so behind."

"Taking charge again?" he teased her.

"I..." She swung her hair back to cascade over her shoulder. "What do you think we should do?"

"We should figure out the lab and the work tomorrow." He pressed the pad to slide their lab door open.

They carefully folded their suits. Thankfully they'd worked as designed, keeping them alive under the worst-case conditions. Harlan plucked one of the blankets from their nest.

Leandra put a hand on his chest as he turned. "I owe you an apology."

"For what?" She'd done nothing wrong.

"I've been controlling and distrusting, and I'm sorry." The sadness in her voice stung. He didn't want his proud, brilliant woman to apologize or compromise. She was amazing just as she was.

"I like the way you are, the way your mind works, your ability to see into the possible future and plan for it." He tucked her hair back and locked his gaze to her soft brown eyes. "You would've made a better leader for the team. But Barret will figure this out and find the right balance. We don't have to own that problem."

"You really think so?"

"Which part?" He couldn't begin to assume he could keep up with her thought processes.

"I would have made a better leader?"

"Absolutely, but I'm glad you aren't." He tugged her into the hallway.

"Why?"

"Because you wouldn't have time for what I intend to do with you."

"Oh?" Her breathy voice had him rushing toward their quarters. "And what's that?"

"Experiments." He opened his door and spun her inside. Dropping the blanket to the side, he guided her backward toward the bed. "*Personal* experiments." He kissed her before she could articulate the question that showed in her eyes. "Fertility experiments."

"You know, I'm an expert in fertility." Her cheeky tone settled low, and his cock filled.

He pressed her shoulders, and she dropped to the bed. "I might need some expert advice."

With a full smile, she reached for his belt, but he stepped back. He trailed a finger over her lower lip. "Beautiful."

He still had a lot to make up for, and he intended to keep her where she was most comfortable, in control. She'd trusted him when the situation was the most dire. She'd relied on him and shown that she could follow his lead. He didn't have to *be* in charge; they could share control. It was his turn to be the most vulnerable, to give her the power. He released the buttons on his shirt, his eyes never leaving hers as he stripped completely naked.

Her gaze roamed his body, and she traced a finger over his abs and around the tip of his cock. "Beautiful."

"I'm yours. Whatever you—"

She tugged his hips forward and guided his cock into her warm wet mouth. All words left him as she sucked him deep. Her grip slid along his shaft. It might have been because they'd faced death hours before, but he'd never been more aware of a moment, more connected to another person, more alive. He threaded his fingers gently through her silky hair, guiding it away from her face so that he could see everything. She lifted her gaze to his, and his knees weakened. He stumbled out of her grip. "I need to see you, all of you."

She stood. "Bed."

That was an order he could follow, even embrace. He sprawled across it and followed each tiny movement as she removed her clothes. Naked as Eve, she stood by the bed, arms at her sides, and he drank her in. His cock twitched against his stomach, demanding, but he waited.

She lifted her knee onto the mattress and shifted to straddle him, once again holding his erection in her soft hand, caressing his length. A teasing spark in her eyes. She was toying with him, but he was content to be with her, no matter what she had planned. Electric shocks spiked along his spine with each downward stroke, and his balls ached with the need to fill her. Unable to remain completely passive, he caressed her thighs, her smooth skin addictive. She rose and guided him to her entrance. His breath caught at the tight heat encasing the tip of his cock. He could thrust his hips, take her, roll her, and fuck her, but damn, the slide of her pussy slowly sinking onto his shaft was a pleasure worth waiting for. He gripped her hips when she settled all the way down, holding her in place but also taking a moment to recover and not give into his body's primitive demands too soon.

She shifted slightly, the sensation as strong as if she'd slammed her hips to his. He closed his eyes to focus on every single nuance of being encased in her wet heat. He blinked when she trailed her fingertips along his cheek.

She smiled. "I love you, Harlan."

"I love you, too, Leandra."

Her pussy clenched his cock in a quick squeeze before she rolled her spine. She rode him, stealing his breath and his sanity. All he could see was her and stars. Unwilling to go before her, he struggled to hold back his release until, finally, she arched her back, her pussy milking the delayed explosion from him and leaving him boneless. Leandra draped herself over him. He wrapped his arms around her, intent on never letting her go again.

Leandra gripped the sheets as Harlan rode her hard from behind, exactly the way she'd commanded him to take her. His grip dug into her hips as he tugged her back and thrust his cock into her begging pussy. Fuck that man filled her perfectly, stretching her walls, bottoming out. His balls smacked against her clit. "Yes!"

"This what you need, love?" he asked in a staccato pulse of words punctuated by his pounding.

"Almost." She was nearly there, the place where he would send her rocketing into the stars. "More."

He sped up his pace, enough to push her over. She dropped her arms, ass held in place, as Harlan continued to work her through her orgasm and then followed her lead into ecstasy. Moments later, he shifted them on the bed, the tingling warm aftershocks still pulsing through her.

"You okay?" His concern radiated through his voice and his gaze as he stroked her rounded belly.

"Mmm-hmm." A fluttery kick met his touch.

"She's active."

"He's hungry," Leandra replied. It had been true since her

fourth month of pregnancy. If she wasn't starving for food, she was ravenous for her husband.

"I'll get some food while you clean up. We're supposed to meet with Shea in less than thirty minutes."

Leandra groaned and shifted off the bed toward the shower, Harlan's cum coating her inner thighs. She loved that he could take the lead, mark her, and it didn't trigger any insecurity. Her trust in him was absolute. He was going to make an amazing father in a few months. The first of the children born to the explorers. Thirty-two of the ships had already connected, and the space station was growing. Mahi and two other doctors had their hands full taking care of the couples who had managed to reproduce with the enhanced fertility protocols Harlan and Leandra had perfected together.

But their baby would be one of the first hybrids born from the zygotes they'd created together.

Harlan guided Leandra to a chair at the conference room table. Scientists filed in, filling every available seat, each greeting Leandra and Harlan by name.

"Thanks for coming, everyone." Shea clicked open files on the computer. "I'm loading the results from the three most promising scenarios." The audience murmured in excited tones. Everyone was eager to move forward with their entire reason for leaving Earth.

"I'll start with the water planet first, as it was the easiest solution in some ways." An image of three planets rotating slowly loaded on the large screen behind her. "Then we can move on to the desert and underground solution. That's going to take some design work to set up domiciles underground and begin altering the soil and atmosphere for farming. Last, we can take up the third planet in our immediate area. That one requires significant resources, and I have several possible solutions that could work."

Leandra glanced out the large window to the stars. The edges of the Cassan space station they called home were visible, the connection ports of the most recently attached ships waiting for the next wave of arrivals. Harlan wrapped his hand around hers, strong and warm. Even though their future was filled with unknowns, she anticipated the coming challenges without a drop of hesitation, only excited for the possibilities.

ACKNOWLEDGMENTS

First, last, and always, thank you to my husband for supporting my writing in every way. I love you!

Thank you to the Red Reines for everything you do!

Thank you to Brandi Doane McCann for another amazing cover.

Thank you to Jenny Rarden for the fantastic editing.

Thank you to my amazing beta readers who made this book infinitely better.

Thank you to Passionate Ink for providing a safe and educational forum for erotic authors.

And thank you to my readers who make writing worth all the struggles!

Award-winning, best-selling author, Jordyn Kross, is an unapologetically naughty novelist who spent years honing her writing skills with tech manuals and marginal poetry before finding her passion for writing sexy, boundary-stretching happily-ever-afters.

When she's not writing, she's attempting to garden in the desert Southwest, hiking with her insane pound posse, and admiring that handsome man wandering around her house who continues to stay.

Jordyn enjoys saucy double entendres, pretending to be an extrovert, and is well-known for having no filter. And when she's not in social media jail, she can be found on Facebook, Instagram, and Bookbub, or hiding in a dark cave peering out at Twitter.

www.ingramcontent.com/pod-product-compliance
Lightning Source LLC
Chambersburg PA
CBHW061548310726
48972CB00008B/2668